CW01483795

CULT
FICTION

Cult Fiction

By
Ardie Collins

KNIGHTSTONE
PUBLISHING

KNIGHTSTONE PUBLISHING

Unit 36,
88-90 Hatton Garden,
London
EC1N 8PN

Published in the United Kingdom by
Knightstone Publishing Ltd
First Published 2011

Copyright © Ardie Collins, 2011

The right of Ardie Collins to be identified as the author of this work has been asserted by him in accordance with the Copyright, Designs and Patents Act 1988.

This book is sold subject to the condition that it shall not, by way of trade or otherwise, be lent, resold, hired out, or otherwise circulated without the publisher's prior consent in any form of binding or cover other than that in which it is published and without a similar condition, including this condition, being imposed on the subsequent purchaser. Enquiries concerning reproduction outside the scope of the above should be sent to the Rights Department, Knightstone Publishing Ltd at the address above.

Cataloguing in Publication Data available

ISBN: 978-1-908134-03-5

Printed and bound by CPI Group (UK) Ltd, Croydon, CR0 4YY

About the Author

Ardie Collins is sometimes hungry and rarely late. He has spent half of his life inhaling and near enough the other half exhaling. He can almost speak one language which is only partly contributable to the fact that he is in the middle of making one up. In between these other commitments he has managed to write a small book.

It's this one, by the way.

Acknowledgements

I am extremely grateful to those that taught me the importance of seeming grateful.

I am also grateful to some more specific people that helped out in various ways towards putting together this debut novel. Anne and Louis Collins (Mum and Dad) for all manner of help, Beth Collins (for naming me) and Georgi Collins (for keeping me in line), Shona Power (for helping out no end), Kim Power (because otherwise she'd feel left out), Aris Tsontzos, Laura Pearce, and Sophie Paterson (for editing help), and all Completely Novel staff (for putting me in the position where I can write acknowledgements). Most people I've ever happened to converse with, most books I've read, most TV shows I've watched, most films I've seen, most radio I've heard, and most music I've listened to have no doubt contributed in some way, though it'd be hard to say exactly how. I'd also like to thank my childhood self for surviving like the trooper he was. Cheers, buddy.

I wrote this book so that I wouldn't go mad, but it ended up making things worse.

For the friends who didn't realise they were helping

A few villagers wondered why Almighty Bob would send his only begotten Sandwich Maker in a burning fiery chariot rather than perhaps in one that might have landed quietly without destroying half the forest, filling it with ghosts and also injuring the Sandwich Maker quite badly. Old Thrashbarg said it was the ineffable will of Bob, and when they asked him what "ineffable" meant, he said look it up.

This was a problem because Old Thrashbarg had the only dictionary and he wouldn't let them borrow it. They asked him why not and he said that it was not for them to know the will of Almighty Bob, and when they asked him why not again, he said because he said so. Anyway, somebody sneaked into Old Thrashbarg's hut one day while he was out having a swim and looked up "ineffable". "Ineffable" apparently meant "unknowable, indescribable, unutterable, not to be known or spoken about." So that cleared that up.

MOSTLY HARMLESS, by Douglas Adams © 1992. Reprinted by kind permission of the Estate of Douglas Adams.

Chapter 1

Then Everything Was Golden

Some people read stories because they offer an escapism that cannot be found elsewhere. Some people read stories because there's been a power cut. The reason you should read this story is because it is very important and I will guide you through it in the pages that follow.

It would be unfair to presume, however, that all those reading are familiar with the idea of a book. Even though it is likely that, to have come this far, one must understand the concept, it would be most undemocratic to make such an assumption. It really is very important for everyone to be able to read everything in this book, so if those that are fine with the idea could be patient for the next paragraph or so, it will really make this whole process a lot easier and we can all set off on the right footing.

Firstly, we shall establish how you gained possession of the book. There are several options, but some of the accepted ones are below:

You bought it.

It was a gift.

You are borrowing it from someone.

You are just scanning it to see if you want to buy it.

You found it perched lovingly underneath a drainpipe.

You stole it.

If your possession relies on the first five categories then I must insist that you stay with me to the end. This is purely because this is all so very important. I can assure you now that it will be extremely worth it. It might not seem like it now but it all gets very exciting. Even by the end of this chapter you will have met the main protagonist, his dog and a destructive fire named Malcolm. If you have stolen this book then I am contractually obliged to encourage you to take it back. But, to be frank, I am always slightly impressed by thieves. It takes guts. And it is somewhat of a skill. Like juggling.

Now we come to how you are to use this book. The basic idea of a book is to be read and the more complex idea of a book is to be understood. We will leave the latter up to someone else for now, although, if you find yourself in such a position then well done, you. Simply make sure that you follow the words left to right along each line, moving down a single line at a time. When you reach the end of the page simply turn it over to reveal a fresh set of words to read. Do remember to remember the first part of each sentence at the end of a page because that sentence will, most likely, continue on the other side of the page. You must understand that I do not intend to be patronising, I just want to make sure we are all on the same page. Luckily, that's this one.

Now then, at the beginning of a story a setting must be established. The setting for the beginning of this particular story is a house. Though this may not seem like an overtly interesting setting, I assure you that the level of interest will increase, perhaps due to the fact that it will burn down very shortly. It was the house of a good and kind man. He's bound to be, at the very least, your second favourite character in this book and if he isn't then I really cannot understand why because he was very pleasant indeed. This man's name was Stephen Moore.

The first thing you must understand about Stephen Moore is that he was very suggestible. The second thing you must understand about Stephen Moore is that he was a Christian. He prayed every night that a man in the sky would aid him through his troubles. This was quite an easy task because he didn't tend to have many troubles. The fact that he did nothing except go to work or church really made the man in the sky's job very easy. And I'm sure he would be eternally grateful. Literally.

Stephen attended his collective every Sunday where they sang to the man in the sky and his son, who is also himself, who once came to Earth, and then died to save us all from ourselves, only to come back to life. It is a gripping tale but I do not have the time to tell it right now as I'm digressing from Stephen's story which, I'm not sure if you are aware, is extremely important. Stephen and his collective sang about all the wonderful things He has done and all the wonderful things He is able to do. Stephen had always felt a certain warmth there amongst all of those people singing about the same thing. But it was not long until the warmth that Stephen enjoyed so much drifted away and left him standing alone and seemingly knowing nothing but cold.

Stephen Moore lived with a dog. He also had two bookshelves, one television set, a DVD player, one computer, seven kitchen cupboards, one cooker, a queen-sized bed, eight pairs of trousers, thirty-two T-shirts, sixteen jumpers, forty pairs of boxer-shorts, forty-two and a half pairs of socks, five pairs of shoes, two suits, three coats, a guitar, a sofa, an alarm clock, a telephone, a CD-player/radio combo, a Frisbee, one-hundred and twenty-four CDs, one-hundred and twenty-three books, fifty-two DVDs, a bottle opener, a can opener, a bag of rice, a bag of pasta, several sauces, a loaf of bread, some chicken, some mince, some butter, some ham, some cheese, some salad leaves, some apples, some dog food (obviously these pieces of food were variable depending on what day it was as

Stephen tended to eat his food and then buy more) a kitchen table, two sinks, one toilet, a shower, and a certain amount of carpet of which I have been unable to ascertain the exact amount. But that doesn't really matter anyway, because all of these things are almost definitely going to be burnt to cinders very soon indeed.

Now that I feel you have gained at least a small understanding of these possessions, I will introduce their owner to you. As is the case with stories, I will not literally introduce him to you. Firstly, I don't know when you'll be reading this and it would be very difficult to guess where you'll be at the time. Secondly, this would be entirely impossible.

Instead of this I will write about him and you may feel as though you have been introduced to him. Perhaps you would like to, metaphorically, stand in the corner of his living room and watch him as he enters through the door. Don't worry, he can't see you.

There he is, walking in through the door. His house was quite cosy, if a little bland. Some people have suggested that Stephen suited his home perfectly. Stephen was a reasonably tall man who wore a tidy side-parting when at work and church and a messy side-parting at other times. His dark hair lay on top of a cheery-looking face that suggested everything was going to be okay, even if it wasn't. He tended to wear suits, except when he bathed, apart from the one time he forgot to take one off. In his leisure time he would also wear clothes.

You can decide what clothing he is wearing at this particular juncture. Make sure you have a good, long think because it is very important and could make the whole story not quite fit into place unless you pick the right outfit. I am almost definitely lying, of course, but 'it's nice to create a bit of tension now and again' as Stephen's mother used to say.

On his arrival home, his small dog, Elijah, would shake his tail vigorously and leap towards Stephen with a certain look on his face that suggested a deep understanding of the concept of an emotional relationship but was actually excitement for the prospect of food.

'It's okay, boy, I'm home now,' was almost always Stephen's response. This would make Elijah's stomach much happier. Stephen would go to the toilet but you don't have to watch that bit. He would then put together some kind of dinner for himself, give Elijah some dinner as well and settle down in front of the television set. He would invariably fall asleep, to be woken up by Elijah licking the small portion of his remaining dinner from his cheek. Stephen would then go to bed, read a small amount of the Bible, rustle up a small prayer and go to sleep with Elijah at the foot of the bed, safe in the knowledge that he would, most definitely, be going to heaven if he happened to die in his sleep.

There is a small amount of irony in this because one night he very nearly did die. And there is almost no way on God's green earth that heaven actually exists, which would have been a nasty shock for Stephen.

So far I have been talking about typical evenings. Let us, instead, move to a definite day of the week. It was a Tuesday. Well, it was very early on a Tuesday. It was actually the night of a Monday but the morning of a Tuesday in that awkward transition point where people don't really know where they are time-wise. Even though it cannot be denied that it was officially a Tuesday as far as the owners of calendar shops are concerned, if you happened to be awake at this time it would not be unreasonable to consider it still part of your Monday.

It's a small period of time where some feel quite alone and others are drenched in an immense feeling of freedom. Various studies into this small period of time have suggested that this is to do with the fact that this is a time when a country's leader is almost definitely asleep. Therefore, those that are fond of their leaders or leadership generally are worried about what might happen over the next few hours. They prefer to tuck themselves up in bed and avoid the whole horrible process of dealing with the thoughts that will begin to form inside their heads about what might happen when the invasion begins. Others, that aren't quite so fond of their leaders or leadership in general, find this an emancipating period of time and use it wisely by running through fields, taking up bewildering hobbies or skinny-dipping in their baths.

This aside, Stephen found himself asleep in the early hours of Tuesday morning, very much and unavoidably minding his own business when, downstairs, a very warm glow was burrowing its way through the house. This warm glow was spreading like wildfire. This was mainly due to the fact that it was a fire called Malcolm and it was spreading rather wildly. He was creeping his way through the household, up the stairs and being generally disruptive along the way. Stephen awoke in a splutter of smoke with a barking dog at the foot of his bed.

Stephen turned on the lamp next to his bed and suddenly sat up, rather rigidly, at the sight of all the smoke. After taking this sight in from a rigid sitting position he thought maybe he should consider it from a standing position. He decided to take forward this idea by standing up very quickly. At first he just stood there, staring oddly at the smoke seeping under his bedroom door. He wondered briefly whether this was a dream. If you were to ask me how I know this then that would very much undermine my position as the narrator. It is essential that you accept that I am aware of, near enough, everything that is going on. There is a two-way trust system occurring here. You must trust me that I am telling you the truth, and I must trust you that you are paying attention. This is mainly due to the fact that this is all very important.

Attention was one of the only things Stephen was capable of at this time as he stood with a gaping mouth while his rather unhelpful mind was asking itself whether it was dreaming. But his wandering, wondering mind which had started to drown out the distant, roaring sound of Malcolm rushing through his house was brought back to consciousness by Elijah's incessant barking.

Once he had returned to the situation, he leapt into action. He quickly grabbed Elijah under his belly, plucked him from the ground and ran to his bedroom door. He opened it and was greeted by a vision of being truly trapped. The roar grew louder and the smoke billowed through the doorway that it had been attempting to seep through for the past few minutes. Malcolm was outside his door and he was very angry. Stephen could see no way around the furious blaze before him and it was up to him to find another way out of the situation.

With great, spluttering difficulty he closed his door and put down his little dog. He scurried over to his window, propped his fingers underneath the groove at the bottom of it and lifted it as wide as possible, staring down into the night's darkness below him. This darkness was his only hope now.

He removed his mattress violently from his bed and forced it out through his bedroom window, hearing a sound that would best be described as the sound of the word 'plump' as it struck the floor. He grabbed Elijah, who had been barking rather unhelpfully throughout this whole situation and made his way back towards the gaping window.

Stephen placed one foot onto the ledge and began to force his way out before his better judgment kicked in and told him to stop. He listened briefly. That is, until his even better judgement reminded him of just how angry Malcolm was and just how behind a wooden door he was. His even better judgement was struggling to overpower his better judgement until his best judgement emerged to clear up the whole situation. His best judgement addressed the squabble by explaining that he would definitely die if he stayed in the bedroom and that mattresses are fairly soft and welcoming. It was this judgement that got things to go its way and Stephen felt himself jump out into the cold, night air.

His stomach lifted out of him as he plummeted towards the mattress. This caused an incomprehensible noise-word to escape from his mouth. The two seconds of falling through the air were the most exciting of Stephen's life, which caused a mixture of distress and shame that Stephen didn't really have time to address right now even though he really, really wanted to. Elijah let out a little whimper as they grew closer to the ground. They found a safe landing on the mattress which they had been sleeping on only minutes before that moment.

Stephen simply lay there for a bit, trying to take in exactly what was going on. Once he realised what there was to take in he thought that perhaps now, more than ever, was the time for a little bit of action. His best judgement agreed so he stood up very quickly from the mattress for the second time in as many minutes. He found his way onto his feet and stepped onto the grass surrounding his house. His feet became instantly entrenched in the cold, wet, dew-ridden grass but this did nothing to make him hesitate. He tried to evoke the sense of being assured as he began walking across the night ground. He forced his hasty breathing to slow gradually as he walked round to the front of his house but soon the situation engulfed him once more and his breathing sped up to an uncontrollable rate when he saw the consuming blaze in front of him. Malcolm was completely and unashamedly ripping apart his house. He began to pace back and forth with his hands gripping various parts of his head entirely unsure of what he should do.

I will be the first to admit that Stephen does not seem to be portraying the qualities of a typical hero but just you wait; he really pulls it out of the bag. He remained there for another minute, though. His bewildered look persisted. His eyes were transfixed on the blaze before him. He was watching Malcolm viciously consume his only home. Billows of smoke slowly wafted into the darkness of the night sky as Stephen's gaze moved up towards the stars.

At this point I have chosen to end this chapter. I find it a sufficiently dramatic moment to make such a decision. Many people like to stop reading at the end of a chapter and take a small break. Others can manage many at once. Other others are quite happy to stop during a chapter and enjoy the challenge of trying to remember the story so far. So you may have already stopped. Other other others (which is the category I fall into) try to take this challenge further and enjoy stopping during a sentence to see how they will cope in two days' time. There are some that enjoy stopping mid-word but those people are quite strange. I would not, however, refuse one round to dinner as I'm sure their minds are fascinating places that I would very much like to explore.

But please take this moment to remove yourself from Stephen's story for a while if you so wish. That is, unless you want to find out what else happens to him right now because the story will almost certainly continue over the page.

Chapter 2

Oranges Are Not A Paradox

W elcome to Chapter 2. I think you will find it most accommodating, which, ironically, is the opposite state of the chapter's main topic of discussion, Stephen's home. To find out the story so far, I refer you to Chapter 1. Unless stated otherwise, the chapters of this story have been set out according to normal numerical order with 'Chapter' written in front of them (i.e. Chapter 1, Chapter 2, Chapter 3, Chapter 4, etc.)

Just to remind you, we left Stephen looking at the stars with a dog in his arms. His expression was not quite one of despair but it was definitely getting there. To break up all this near-despair, he took a moment to thank God very much indeed for his survival. He was struggling slightly with why this had happened to him and why he wasn't able to still be asleep in bed. He longed for the very recent past. There were moments when the bizarre nature of the situation assured him that this must be a dream but the mere fact that he was able to think that assured him that it almost certainly wasn't.

His head was bulging with questions. Metaphorically speaking, of course. His head was not physically bulging with questions. If it were then my advice to him would be to stop asking questions because they're making his head bulge. But now was not the time for head-bulging, it was time to actually do something about the current situation. He ran next door for some good, old-fashioned Christian charity.

He made the six second walk to his neighbour's door. It seemed like a lifetime. It wasn't of course. It actually lasted seven seconds if you must know. But it certainly wasn't a lifetime, apart from maybe to some kinds of single-cell bacteria or certain radioactive chemicals. Come to think of it, a lifetime is a purely subjective thing depending on whose lifetime is being considered. So, if Stephen felt that it took a lifetime then that's his choice. It didn't, of course.

He arrived at the door and raised his hand in a fist. Every time that Stephen moved his fist in a quick movement and struck the door of his neighbour's house he created a knock. He wasn't showing off or anything; it was just something he had almost always been able to do as far back as he could remember. Stephen made a knock four times in reasonably quick succession. He was normally a three-knock man and he very much prided himself on that fact but the current situation warranted a slightly more urgent sounding knock. He even made his usual thirty-second gap between knocking sessions (which is only polite in normal situations) a mere five seconds. There was a slight pang in his conscience as he did this as, even now, as his house was burning down, it didn't quite feel right.

Soon there came a clattering of movement from the other side of the door as an old woman by the name of Phyllis Entwhistle fumbled down the stairs. Her glazed eyes were the first things that greeted Stephen's as she peered through the partially open door.

'Stephen?' she muttered sleepily, 'is that you, son?'

'Yes, Mrs Entwhistle. Sorry to have woken you, it's just that...'

'Sorry, I didn't recognise you without my glasses. Hang on, I'll just get them. Come on through.'

'That's not really necessary, Mrs Entwhistle. I've just come over because...'

'No. No problem, dear. I'll just pop off and get them. You've obviously something very important to tell me, coming over here at half past four in the morning or at this time of night. Is it today or tomorrow?' he heard her slowly mumbling to herself as she went to get her glasses.

Stephen made his way through the doorway of the living room. He simply stood politely for a moment and looked around the room at the various trinkets. The wallpaper was covered in repeated images of oranges hanging from, presumably, orange trees. He assured himself that he would feel no anger at all if the oranges were inaccurately hanging from oak trees as the main issue troubling him at the present moment was the fiery predicament he was in and, instead of simply standing in a living room with wallpaper that may or may not be botanically accurate, he should be phoning for the fire-brigade.

'Actually, Mrs Entwhistle?' he bellowed politely down the hallway.

'Yes, dear?' came the faint reply of the old lady.

'I just came over to ask if I could borrow your phone quickly. I need to phone the fire brigade. My house is…'

'Sorry, dear. Can't quite hear you from here. I'd better get my hearing do-whatsit as well before I come back down to hear your important news.'

'That really won't be necessary, Mrs Entwhistle,' he called again. 'I just need to borrow…'

'Hold on, dear.'

Stephen could see the fire consuming more and more of his house in his head as the seconds ticked by waiting for an old lady to find her replacement senses. He very much liked Mrs Entwhistle but she was only useful in certain situations. She was very useful, for example, if one had a few hours to spare and one didn't really know what to do with oneself and one felt like a chat about nothing much whatsoever over a cup of tea. She was not a very good person to have around, however, if all of one's worldly possessions were being eaten up by flames. We all have our strengths and weaknesses, I suppose.

So, while Mrs Entwhistle was searching upstairs for her glasses, Stephen began searching downstairs for the telephone. The house was immaculate. There were no piles of things covering other things (the usual location of a lost phone) or vast layers of items clinging to one another against a wall. He was having no luck at all in locating the telephone in this serene environment of unadulterated cleanliness.

He began scurrying around the ground floor of the house. He ran into the kitchen to find entirely empty kitchen counters. Mrs Entwhistle packed everything away, even her toaster, if it was not in use. The only other room he hadn't been in was the toilet, though he risked the prospect of being found to be extraordinarily wrong by not bothering to look in there. He returned to the living room which contained a small television set, a bookshelf being put to its recognised purpose and some bewildering ornaments of various animals, people and children. He didn't want to be caught searching the house when Mrs Entwhistle returned as he felt that would be slightly rude so he resigned himself to failure and simply waited patiently for her return.

The slow trundle of an old lady's footsteps were coincidentally aligned with an old lady, donned with spectacles and hearing aids, walking down some stairs so Stephen assumed an atmosphere of calm in the living room where she had left him. His surface was very much belying the emotions beneath.

'Now, Stephen,' she said as she wandered through the living room door, 'what brings you here?'

'Well, actually, I just needed to...'

'Cup of tea, son?'

'No thanks, Mrs Entwhistle.'

'You wouldn't take a sandwich, I assume,' she said.

'No. Thanks, though. I just needed...'

'Only I made one earlier and couldn't really finish it. I cut it and everything. It's in the fridge; I can go and get it if you want. Just wait...'

'No, Mrs Entwhistle. I'm fine, really. I need to borrow your phone, my house is on fire.'

'Your house is what, dear?'

'On fire.'

'Good God!' she said, 'well, have you phoned the fire-brigade?'

'No, I was hoping you could help me with that. My phone's in my burning wreck of a house, you see. If I could just use yours that would be fantastic.'

'Of course, of course. It's just there, son.' She pointed with her aging finger over at the windowsill where a phone in the shape of a dog was sitting obediently. He had not thought that this dog disguised among various other ornaments was the phone at any moment during his search and he immediately leapt at it in excitement. He lifted off its back and dialled for some form of help.

It is a curious thing, rage. It alters a person. Or perhaps that's slightly unfair, surely rage is an emotion and we cannot blame it any more than we can blame marmalade for being orangey. When I say that 'rage alters a person' it makes rage the active participant. It is much fairer to say that a person is altered when they choose rage. I say this because Stephen chose rage after finding that Mrs Entwhistle's telephone didn't do exactly what it's supposed to. The requirement he reasonably expected of it was the ability to phone people. It turned out that it was no more than an ornament. A hideous, plastic, happy, stupid, dog-faced ornament with a wire sticking out of it that had burrowed its way into a wall where the phone service had never been connected.

Stephen, however, being the kind person that he is (I mentioned earlier that you'd like him very much) did not take out any of his rage on Mrs Entwhistle. She was a confused old lady, after all. Rather, Stephen masked his rage until he had thanked Mrs Entwhistle (this would, sadly, be the last time he'd see her in a vertical position) and left quietly via her front door carrying little Elijah with him. His rage was let out in a kind of primal scream, which he felt all the better for. The scream wasn't aimed at anyone in particular; it was more of a release because of the hideous nature of the whole situation.

After this small interlude of anger-venting, Stephen returned to himself and he moved relatively quickly in the direction of his other neighbour on the other side of his house. To do this, of course, he had to pass his burning home once more. He tried not to look too much but he did anyway. The flames were definitely worse.

He knocked on his other neighbour's door at that early hour of the morning or late hour of the night, if you'd prefer, and I will tell you what happened in the next chapter.

Chapter 3

And They All Went Fifth

Nothing. Nothing happened. He was on holiday. Pity to waste a chapter, though. I'll tell you about something else. The teachings of Mooranity tell us that The Platinum Staircase is only available for access once we are ready for death. They also tell us that a man with a magic guitar plectrum once played a peasant's ukulele so loud that it could be heard in Australia. The teachings of Mooranity, collated in a book entitled 'Just Some Thoughts On How We Should Live Our Lives', neglect to tell us where the man that played this ukulele was which is a shame because it is certainly very impressive if the man was in Germany but not quite so impressive if he was actually already in Australia at the time. However, these trivial matters are largely unimportant; the message of the teachings is what is most crucial.

Teachers of Mooranity tend to get a little hot under the collar when you try to pick holes in the story of The Platinum Staircase and its origin or try and explain that there is little to no meaning to the Love, Peace, Happiness and Goldfish prayer. It's best not to do that when you're standing next to one of them, I suppose.

Stephen Moore was trapped in the night time, running towards the next house, hoping it would have a functioning telephone inside it. He knocked sheepishly on its door. Eventually a woman answered, her eyes desperate to close and her brain telling her otherwise.

'What is it, Stephen?' she tried to say calmly.

'Hi Wendy. My house is on fire. Could I borrow your telephone?'

'Oh my God! Of course you can. Yes, yes, come in, come in.'

He did.

He rushed towards the phone that was hanging on the wall of the kitchen and picked it up much quicker than one normally would. His heart became as relieved as it possibly could have been in the given situation when he heard a dialling tone. 'Thank Christ!' he shouted quite violently as he dialled '999'. He informed them, as calmly as possible, that his house was on fire and that he would like a fire engine to pop over nice and quickly.

After having phoned for the fire brigade, it was simply a case of waiting.

'They said they'd be around as soon as possible. Is it alright if I wait here until then?'

'Of course, Stephen. Jesus. Do you know how it happened?'

'No. I can't think of anything I left on and I'm almost certain that I didn't leave any petrol around.' He was trying to make the situation slightly lighter. It worked a bit. He found a seat in Wendy's living room armchair.

Wendy was a 40-something woman whose eyes told stories of a messy divorce. Once again, I don't want metaphors to get muddled. Wendy's eyes didn't *actually* tell stories of a messy divorce. They would have to be very talented eyes indeed and if they could tell stories it would be good if they changed it around a bit rather than just telling the same story about the same messy divorce over and over again. Especially if they were to talk about Wendy's because Wendy's ears would invariably hear this story from them all the time and this would make her very upset indeed. So, her eyes, metaphorically speaking, told a story that suggested that Wendy had been one half of a tale that was based around a messy divorce. She had long, dark hair that was quite fuzzy at the moment because she had just been woken up by a man whose house was on fire. She was quite thin, and stood with an air of calm that suggested that even if something was about to happen, she already knew about it and had some extra life-jackets.

'Can I get you anything, Stephen?' said the calm voice from the woman in the cotton dressing gown.

'Actually, yeah. Could I possibly have a cup of tea? Lots of sugar, please. Thanks, Wendy.'

'No problem,' she said as she wandered off to the kitchen. Elijah sat on the windowsill watching the darkness outside. A small glow continued to penetrate this darkness and, even though Stephen's house could not be seen from this window, Malcolm's presence could still be felt in this unwelcome glow.

Stephen remained in the armchair, unsure of whether he should be comfortable or not. The basis of this lack of assuredness stemmed from him not knowing whether to put his arms on the arms of the chair or to remain with his hands on his lap, in the position of a nervous 7-year-old who was about to tell his auntie that he had just broken her greenhouse with a football. He decided to ignore either of these options and instead to slowly lower himself into the armchair. His house was on fire; wasn't he allowed to relax if he wanted to?

As he sat, he thought. He thought about how he had found himself thinking a lot more since the mattress and fire incident. He felt quite different. He couldn't quite put his finger on it, mostly because it was a conceptual thought process and not something anyone could possibly put their finger on but also because he'd never felt this feeling before as far back as his memory served. Just before he realised something that will become very important for the rest of this story, Wendy returned with his cup of tea and a couple of biscuits to put off this crucial turning point until the end of the chapter at least.

Stephen slowly emptied his mug using the traditional method of sipping. He had momentarily forgotten about his flame-related problem during a discussion about Elijah's latest trick but this mindless chatter was suddenly interrupted by a chiming telephone. It was Wendy's. She gave a curious look to Stephen as if to say, 'that's strange; another person at this hour of the night?' Stephen gave a look back as if to say, 'or the morning, of course. Anyway, yes, you should probably answer your telephone. It has rung four times now. Yes, best to head around to the left side of the table, there we go.' But Wendy missed the final portion of his look as she was busy picking up the telephone.

One of the problems with telephone calls (and there are many) is that a bystander only gains half of the conversation. This is, of course, a mostly positive thing if the conversation is intended to be a private one. However, when someone's house is on fire and the person that has answered the phone is called Wendy and she is giving sideways glances towards the victim of the burning house called Stephen then it isn't so great. Obviously this is not an overly common situation (only 0.00015% of the human population of the world have experienced it) but it is still worth mentioning. I wouldn't want to be accused of needless exclusivity.

'Hello?' Wendy said. The caller said something. 'Oh, yes, that's right,' said Wendy. The caller said something. 'Right,' said Wendy. The caller said something. 'I see,' said Wendy. The caller said something. 'Okay. That's fine. Yes, I'll tell him,' said Wendy. The caller might have said something but Wendy would not have heard it because she had placed the telephone back down.

You see my point from this conversation, I suspect. We've only gained half the information involved, if that. The only thing we can conclude from this telephone conversation is that Wendy is, at the very least, feigning understanding of a certain situation. I suspect Wendy will probably begin to tell Stephen exactly what she had gleamed in less than a moment.

'Stephen. I'm afraid I have some rather bad news. I see you're already sitting down. The fire engine you called for has broken down. But they're sending another one.'

It is a curious thing, rage. For a full understanding of that reference see the previous chapter.

The normal inclination of Stephen's rage was to remain internalised and to not directly affect many of those around him. This normal inclination was followed as Stephen said no more to Wendy but instead found himself rushing down the road to his burning home and watching as the flames consumed the previously intact property.

He had felt compelled to witness it pull down the vestiges of his physical memories. He would look away in horror and grasp the top of his head with his hands in disbelief but he would always uncontrollably turn to look, only to repeat the cycle over and over again.

He was close to tears. The flames were full of blame. The blame was aimed at the old lady who didn't understand telephones and the neighbour who always seemed to be around but went on holiday for the first time in their life yesterday evening. And the fire sergeant who sent out an unreliable fire engine. But, really, he didn't blame any of them. The old lady obviously didn't burn his house down nor did she intend to. The neighbour obviously needed a break from whatever job she does and the fire engine scenario was just, as many happy-go-lucky people say, one of those things. Many people also use this phrase to describe objects that they can't quite remember the name of but these two uses are mostly unrelated.

But soon his blame moved to much larger, more bearded things. He blamed God. And then he felt guilty. And then he wondered why he should. And then he felt guilty again. And then he took a full step back from the whole situation. And with the fluttering flames disappearing into the sky above him and the smoke lifting to nowhere, he could see his rage disappear too and with it, it took his faith.

Chapter 4

Disgust and Anger and Chocolate

We've come quite far now, haven't we? Once again we find ourselves at a new chapter. But, for a general round-up, see the last sentence of the previous chapter. Obviously that single sentence does not include all of the various exciting plot lines but it does sum up quite nicely what is occurring around our lovely protagonist at this moment in the story.

Stephen continued to stare at the flames rising and blending into the darkness. He watched the smoke drifting into a sky that, until about thirty seconds ago, he believed to contain a heavenly paradise. He lowered himself onto the curb opposite his house and, as he sat on his little spot, he thought.

He felt different. He wasn't quite sure how to describe it or articulate it or even think about it but he definitely felt different. His soul felt strange. But he soon realised that it was his stomach that felt strange or a region around his stomach. This seemed too much, too fast but it was too immediate in his mind to completely dismiss. What he really wanted to do now was to go home and have a good, long think about himself. And he would have, it wasn't exactly far to walk, it was just that his home seemed to be rather hot and crumbly at the moment in question. Hot and crumbly are not very hospitable properties for a house when someone wants to go home and have a good, long think, as I'm sure you'll agree.

So he decided to have a good, long think with his dog on his lap, sitting on the pavement opposite his house, waiting for the second fire engine to arrive. As he sat in his pyjamas, his thoughts changed rapidly, quickly skipping between things that began to make sense before disappearing just out of reach. His biggest worry was how he was going to tell his mother but then he remembered that she was dead. Then he worried about telling his father and then he remembered, horribly, that he was still alive. He decided the best thing would be to never tell him. 'That should be easy enough,' he thought, 'I only see him at Christmas and everyone's a Christian at Christmas.' Then he thought about whether he should still go to church. The obvious thought would be 'No, what's the point now?' but he also worried about what everyone would think if he stopped.

Then he worried about what he'd do with himself, generally. He went to church every week and apart from his job he didn't get up to much else. Again, you must rely on me to relay all of this information to you. Trust me; I know he was thinking all of these thoughts. Admittedly, there are a lot of thoughts for me to have remembered but the beauty is that I don't have to remember as such, I simply know these events in Stephen's mind to be true. At least I think I do.

He thought perhaps there was some collective for people like him and if there wasn't then perhaps he could start something up. But now was not the time both in terms of his house being in immediate danger of disappearing altogether and because of the fact that it was that awkward transition point between evening and morning when you didn't know exactly what day you'd call it. Just as he resolved to stop thinking about it, a deafening scream came down the street that would almost certainly have interrupted his thoughts anyway. The fire engine had arrived. Stephen stood up and watched as the fire-fighters began putting out the fire that had removed Stephen's possessions from him. They were exceptionally calm. This made Stephen feel a little better. The hoses gushed out watery-foam that sent steam up into the sky as it struck the burning blaze. Slowly, Malcolm began to become a little calmer and a little smaller until, bit by bit, he entirely disappeared.

All of this is reasonably exciting and very important, of course, but I also need to tell you about something else that had happened down the street about an hour earlier. Stephen was making his way steadily through another seemingly undisturbed sleep and this is not wholly irrelevant to the new event I'm going to tell you about if I can just find a suitable way to end this sentence. About twenty houses along from the house that Stephen was sleeping in there were two young boys who were also meant to be sleeping. They were having a sleepover and had crept out of the house in the middle of the night for a game that they called 'midnight marbles'. They had cleverly called it this because they had come up with the ingenious idea of employing the rules and apparatus of marbles (which included marbles mostly) and playing it in the middle of the night. They were shocked to see a man walking past smoking a cigarette. They froze on the path outside the house, frightened of whether he'd tell the adults inside, and just generally frightened as children sometimes tend to be. But the man simply walked past without appearing to notice them. He disappeared around the bend of the street closely followed by the smoke he had created from his mouth.

The boys had just settled on a perfect spot to play when something caught their attention down the street, it was a small, bright, orange glow and a miniscule stream of smoke rising into the atmosphere and, in total disregard of the international marble rules which clearly state that competitors cannot leave a game half way through even if they really need the toilet, they wandered down the street to find out what was going on.

As they approached it, they realised that it was a small fire that was collecting outside of a house. It was called Malcolm. They had waited their entire lives (which, so far, had been quite short) for this. They were to be heroes. One of the boys proclaimed that his Dad had a watering can in the garage. They quickly scurried under the cover of darkness to grab it. As they opened the garage door as quietly as possible the boy who lived in the house turned on the light. The dingy garage slowly flickered into visibility as the bulb struggled into action as though surprised and a little irate by such a request at this hour. They spotted the desired plastic can slumbering against the back wall. The boy whose father owned the can clambered over a few old bikes and some discarded furniture to grab it. It was full. This surprised him slightly but also made his heroics a little easier. He clambered back over to the garage entrance, careful not to spill anything on the disused furniture and filthy floor. It was this boy that insisted he carry the can to the fire.

They ran back down the road, the liquid inside sloshing back and forth and proving heavier than the boy originally thought. He decided to let the other boy have a go at carrying it as well.

'Smells a bit funny, doesn't it?' said one to the other.

'Yeah. It's just old,' said the other, very insistent that he knew exactly what was going on because he was definitely cleverer than his friend. They eventually arrived in front of the small flame. It was barely up to much at all, just minding its own business and being generally quite hot. Both boys grabbed hold of their newly acquired container, ready to prove that they were brave.

'Let's save the day!' one of the boys said as they pulled it backwards and then lunged forwards. They stopped the container just in front of the flame so that the liquid could flow out of the spout in an arc and onto Malcolm. The petrol which had just landed on Malcolm suddenly made him quite angry and this made the boys do what any self-respecting children would do in the situation. They ran home.

You might think that the inclusion of this side-story from around an hour earlier is raising further questions of blame or determinism or free will or things like that. But it is simply there because that's what happened. I really wouldn't want anyone to read too much into it. That might lead to a dark and dreary place and I'm not entirely sure that you'd get out again.

Chapter 5

The Idea Shuddered Back

Wendy offered Stephen a place to stay while his house was being rebuilt. That place was her house in case you were unsure. It is generally considered to be very rude to offer someone else's house as a place to stay, especially without asking them first. It is also considered rude to begin to offer someone a place to stay and then offer them instructions to the nearest hotel. But it is even ruder to offer someone a place to stay and then to ask them, 'Why? What's wrong with your place?' immediately after their house has burnt down before their eyes.

Wendy had wandered down the road in her dressing gown and offered Stephen a bed for the remaining hours of the night. Stephen had gratefully accepted but, without looking away from the sight before him, said something along the lines of 'yeah, I'll just, mhmm, thank, yeah, I'm just going to, you know. Thanks, Wendy.' And he continued to watch his flame-riddled house being tackled by the fire-fighters. In case Stephen's speech confused you just then, it is probably because Stephen's mind was confusing itself at the time. He was very distressed and depressed and he couldn't help but digress (That rhymed. How brilliant). I can only report things as they happened, otherwise that wouldn't be very fair to anyone. Anyway, I'm 76% certain that that is exactly what Stephen said.

Eventually, however, after receiving some instructions from the fire-fighters that he didn't fully understand because of the dilapidated state of his mind, he thanked them graciously and made his way back to Wendy's house.

It was a nice enough house and this act of kindness would definitely rank her as currently my favourite character in this story. Obviously, your own personal ranking is up to you. Perhaps you could take some time to write down the pros and cons of each character we've met so far. These are Stephen, Elijah, Malcolm, Mrs Entwhistle, the neighbour, Wendy, the fire sergeant, a collection of fire-fighters, Stephen's dead mother and alive father, a man with a cigarette and the two marble boys. On the other hand, that was only an option for those that were struggling to keep up with the comings and goings of the people relevant to Stephen's story. For those that are feeling fine about all that then it really is quite important that you keep reading and hear about Stephen and the events that surround him.

Wendy was waiting for him with another cup of tea as he arrived at the front door. Very little was said for the next twenty minutes and anything that was said was said very carefully as though the words might shatter as they struck the floor. A collective decision was made through gestures alone that it was time to go to bed.

In Wendy's spare room, Stephen's mind was not as dilapidated as it previously had been but he did find himself lying there wide-eyed and entirely unable to get to sleep. He was blinking much less than a normal person. But his mind was racing very much like a... well, a racehorse I suppose. If that simile did not suffice then I can only apologise, if you feel you can think of a better one, which is highly likely, then simply write your alternative in the provided space below. That way, if you ever read this again or you lend it to a friend/family member then they can appreciate it that little bit more. Anyway, his mind was racing like...........................* at Ascot Racecourse and his thoughts were spiralling in and around and over one another.

'How can bad things happen to good people?' remained one of his biggest thoughts. He used to be told such things as, 'It's all part of a larger plan we can't understand'. He thought that was rather mysterious but then, of course, 'God moves in mysterious ways' was his mind's response to this. 'Enough!' he thought. If you could hear his thoughts it would have been

---

*   Insert your simile here.

some kind of sudden and unexpected shout in a sea of calm.
Also, if you could hear his thoughts, I would be very impressed.
He decided it was probably best to go to sleep, but this was
entirely impossible. Perhaps he could think himself to sleep.
He was somewhat boring himself with all these repetitive
thought-arguments but they were just making him a little
uncomfortable and nervous. It's understandable. Everything
he'd ever thought seemed to have been stolen from him. To
make it worse and more confusing, he had stolen it himself, he
wasn't sure where he'd put it and he wasn't sure what should
go in its place. This was much too fast but he resolved that
tomorrow was a new day, which is both very wise and very
obvious.

One way or another, Stephen drifted off to sleep. His key
tactics involved closing his eyes and remaining still. His
contorted and tense mind relaxed and it began to enter into
dream worlds.

Most of Stephen's dreams that night involved fire in some
way. One of the most vivid involved him clambering through
the darkness and lifting himself over the ridge of the top of a
cliff. Standing in front of him was a burning bush that began
talking to him. The conversation went something like this:
   'I have something very important to tell you, Stephen.'
   'Really? Because from where I'm standing, you're a bush.
How important could news from a bush be?'

'That is merely your perception of things. To your eyes I am simply a bush but I am so much more than that.'

'Well what are you then? Actually, don't worry, I'm off. I can't be bothered with this.'

'No, wait. Come back here when I'm talking to you. I demand you to return. Dammit! Why did I choose a bush? There's no way a bush evokes authority.'

Stephen's dream-self was hardly listening to the final moments of the fiery bush scorning itself before he found that the darkness had turned to blissful daytime and he was walking down a green hillside.

He found his way into a field. He became surrounded by the kind of pastures that can only exist in dreams and false memories. Cows seemed to drift into the air to let him through as he continued to walk across the verdant fields. He was free, he was without cares and, as a consequence, he was carefree when suddenly a loud, rumbling voice broke through the silent air and rang loudly in Stephen's head.

'Get out!' shouted the rumbling voice.

'What? Who said that?' inquired Stephen.

'Never mind who it is! I'm in charge around here. Now get out!'

'But I'm having a nice time. What do you mean get out? How can I get out?'

'Just get OUT!' rumbled the voice once more. The sheer force of the voice forced him to fall to the ground. As he fell, his instinct to put his hands out arrived and Stephen found himself suddenly waking up with a start, a rush of adrenaline leaving him frightened and alert. It took him a moment to establish that he wasn't falling and relief washed through his veins. As soon as he realised it was all a dream and that he was safe in bed and not being harassed by burning bushes or faceless, bellowing voices he returned to the pillow and drifted back to sleep.

Stephen awoke. And then he went back to sleep again. Stephen awoke properly and had that strange sensation one gets when one wakes up in a strange environment. It was not that Wendy's spare room was strange (particularly if you looked beyond the extensive collection of porcelain kittens), it was just new for Stephen in the morning. At first he thought, 'Where am I?' and then he remembered. And then he thought, 'Yes, but why am I here?' and then he remembered and this caused him to let out a kind of humphy groan and he rolled over as the memory of last night's burning-related events came flooding back.

Perhaps 'flooding' is the wrong term here as the one time when Stephen may have welcomed a flood would have been during the time his house was on fire. Obviously that would mean his house would get very wet but perhaps an over-sized towel could mop that up. Then again, perhaps an over-sized towel would have been good to douse the flames during the fire. Come to think of it, there are a lot of situations where over-sized towels are the answer. Another situation when over-sized towels would be the answer is on a game show where the question was, 'What cotton-based item employs a prefix that has an alternative meaning to 'large' or 'vast' and could be used in both excessively fiery and excessively wet situations?' But after that small set of pointless thoughts Stephen rolled out of Wendy's spare bed and headed down towards the place where the smell of toast was coming from.

Wendy greeted him standing near the kettle. The kettle was on, which was very useful given Stephen's desire for a cup of tea.

'Oh, good morning, Stephen,' said Wendy as she noticed him coming through the kitchen door, 'Would you like a cup of tea? Or some toast?'

'I'll take both if it's not an either/or question.'

'No, no, of course not. Grab yourself some of that toast out of the toaster. Sugar and milk in your tea?'

'Both, please.'

As the breakfast was being made Wendy inquired about whether Stephen would be going to work. He responded with his voice.

'I just don't think I'm ready for it. I think I'm going to take a couple of days just to sort all of this out.'

'Absolutely. I think you need to just take some time. It's not every day that people have to deal with their house burning down.'

They sat down at the kitchen table where they both found it extremely difficult to move the conversation away from Stephen's burnt down house. They tried talking about the lost cat that they'd seen on the posters dotted around the area. They tried talking about how difficult it is to remove your coat when sitting down next to strangers you don't want to accidentally touch. They even tried talking about important events from around the world that had cropped up on the radio in the kitchen. But, alas, none of these topics could distract enough so they ended up just talking about what would most likely happen next in the story of Stephen's burnt down house.

'My house has never burnt down before,' said Stephen.

'Nor mine,' added Wendy rather unhelpfully.

'No, I wasn't trying to compare, I was simply saying that my house has never burnt down before so I don't know what I should do next.'

'Oh, I see,' said Wendy, 'nor do I, I'm afraid. Perhaps begin with the insurance company?' Which is what Stephen did.

I'll be perfectly honest; this portion of Stephen's tale is decidedly unexciting. I just feel that telling you about his laborious phone-calls to his insurance company (the company that couldn't get around the fact that the forms he needed were burnt down in the house that he was making his claim about) would be very boring indeed. He listened to Vivaldi's 'Four Seasons' for what felt like five seasons. Eventually, something or other was sorted out. It's largely unimportant to the rest of the story and I lost interest half-way through his phone-call so I won't bore you with any of it. It's not as if I told you every one of Stephen's dreams during his night's sleep. If I was to carry on down that road then I would be saying things like 'Stephen breathed in and stepped with his left leg down towards his home that was on fire then he stepped with his right leg then his left leg then he started to breathe out just as he placed his right foot down again,' and this whole process would take a very long time indeed. All I will say is that the phone-call was a nightmare and, by the time he had put the phone down, Stephen got pretty far away but close enough to what he had wanted when he had picked it up all those hours ago that he was in a state that could vaguely be referred to as satisfaction. Wendy arrived home from work around this time.

'I'll see you alright for the massive phone bill you're going to get from today,' Stephen told Wendy after the usual conversational pleasantries.

'That's fine, Stephen. And, just so you know, you're fine to stay here as long as you need.'

'Thanks Wendy,' he said, 'that means a lot.'

Stephen spent the next few days not doing very much at all. He would intend to tidy up Wendy's house a little bit at a time each day to make up for staying there but he would somehow be surrounded by an inordinate amount of mess with his feet up, watching bad television programmes about boring people when she walked in through the door from work every day. He would feel guilty, explain himself, resolve to not do it again the next day and find himself inevitably in the same position again. One evening, Wendy was reading a book whilst Stephen hurried around her tidying up his mess for the day. Though they were both doing tasks, they managed to talk to one another.

'Maybe you should find some kind of a hobby, Stephen', said Wendy without looking up from her book or losing her place in the story. Stephen was balancing several plates in one hand whilst wiping a cloth over a table with his other hand.

'Yeah. I think you're right, Wendy,' he said, 'I was thinking about that, but I don't really know what. I'm not very sporty or sociable or artistic or adventurous.'

'Maybe Extreme Team Tennis Painting?' was Wendy's offer.

'Maybe,' said Stephen, 'but I was thinking about something I have been thinking quite a bit about since my house burnt down.'

There was a silence. Wendy carried on looking at her book for a bit but, eventually, in the middle of a word, she looked up and said, 'Well, are you going to tell me or is the plate balancing a clue?'

'Oh. Right. Yeah', were some of Stephen's noises as he increased the pile of plates and began dusting a television. 'Well. I had a kind of revelation. After the whole fiery thing a couple of days back.'

'I think I remember.'

'Well, it sort of made me a little more questioning of God and His motives and that kind of thing.'

'How do you know it wasn't just some kids with a petrol tank?'

Stephen paused, took a moment and then responded, 'Well. I don't. But then that brings me to the same conclusion, doesn't it?'

'How do you mean?'

'Well, either God was pointlessly causing a fire to go through my house and burn all of my possessions even though I'm a good Christian, suggesting he's a malicious creature, which is not what we're taught about him so the one I know doesn't exist. Or it was just some kids who were playing marbles and got hold of a petrol tank so God didn't do it and nor did he stop it, which also suggests that he's not the one I know and so doesn't exist.'

'Suppose you're right there,' said Wendy as she returned to the second part of the word she had left a moment ago. 'So how does this relate to your hobby of choice?'

'Well, I was thinking that this has been a bit of a shock to the system and perhaps there are others like me who have recently lost everything they fundamentally believed in. It hasn't been easy but I thought that maybe I'd start some kind of support group or something and we could help each other out.'

'That's a really good idea.' And then she looked up from her book. 'I hope it works out well and it doesn't go horribly wrong and end up being something to write about one day.'

Stephen wasn't entirely sure that he had got to grips with Wendy's humour yet but he still forced out a small chuckle and sat down to watch the television a little more before bed. He resolved that he would begin planning his support group in the morning.

Stephen woke up both nice and early the next day and began planning his group for those that have lost their faith. He walked over to the phone and felt an all-over shuddering feeling as he had not had a good relationship with phones over the past couple of days and had possibly gained a not wholly irrational fear of them.

But he managed to pluck up the courage and he phoned the local community centre to see how he would go about booking the hall for an evening. They told him that it was best to phone them. He then realised that he was already doing that so he decided to book a Friday night at the centre. He then asked for the address to send the money to. They told him. He asked how much it was and they told him it was free. He asked what the point was in giving the address to send the money to when there was no need to send any money. They said they weren't sure. Eventually Stephen managed to hang up the phone and he set about making the flyers and posters to advertise it.

He'd always enjoyed arts and crafts-related things at school but he was never very good. He would often find he had more things stuck to himself than the paper he was working on but this was hardly exceptional. Kids are stupid.

The feeling of setting his mind to a project he might actually enjoy came back to him as he sat at the coffee table drawing up his posters. They ended up reflecting Stephen's character in that they weren't very exciting at all but gave all the information that was required:

HAVE YOU RECENTLY LOST YOUR FAITH?

THIS IS A SUPPORT GROUP DEDICATED TO PEOPLE LIKE YOU WHO ARE CONFUSED, LOST, OR EVEN HAPPY WITH THEIR NEW WAY OF THINKING!

IF YOU'D LIKE TO TALK TO LIKE-MINDED PEOPLE ABOUT SUCH ISSUES THEN COME ALONG TO THE COMMUNITY CENTRE EVERY FRIDAY AT 7PM

Contact Stephen Moore on 07---------

I thought it best to conceal Stephen's phone number. I think that I'm already prying into Stephen's life quite enough by telling you what he's been dreaming about and one has to draw a line somewhere.

Stephen put the posters up everywhere, as people would say, but that is not even a tiny bit true. When you think about how big the world is and the blip of existence that is Stephen Moore, he didn't put them up at all, let alone everywhere. But if we are to return to our insular state of mind then Stephen did, indeed, put them up everywhere in his local area. Again, if we are to consider the size of the posters and the twenty he put up in his local area and how little space they take up we are not even getting anywhere remotely close to everywhere but he did put them up on trees and windows and walls.

He had a cheery skip in his step as he did this. The sun was shining and his mind was off his burnt down house for the first time in a couple of days but then thinking about the fact that he wasn't thinking about it managed to bring it all back and the skip in his step became decidedly trudgey. He soon ran out of posters just as the gathering rainclouds gave up on trying to hold all of that water and they let it all fall to earth. He managed to make it home before the rain had fully soaked through the layer of clothing closest to his skin but this was little consolation and the saying 'every cloud has a silver lining' was either not applicable or far too applicable in the given situation and Stephen didn't really want to think about which one it was.

This has been a pretty long chapter in relation to the other ones so far. If you found it hard going then I can only apologise but I hope that you've remembered my advice from Chapter 1 because that should make it a little bit easier. And it really is very important that you're able to keep up. You could take a little break or you could continue reading as things will start to make a little more sense. So far, I think that it has all been nicely set up for the plot to thicken. I could not tell the whole story in one sentence, otherwise all the important details would be missed out. But if I were to try, it would be this sentence: Oh dear.

Chapter 6

Their Insides Were Gone

Stephen took a small trip around to his house. The one that had horribly burned down at exactly the same time as Malcolm had rushed through it. You would be forgiven for thinking that there was a very small possibility that Stephen's house burning down and the fire that ruthlessly rushed through it on the same night were an unfortunate coincidence and that there was no direct correlation between the two. However, it has become clear, due to undeniable evidence, that Malcolm the fire was the guilty one in this whole mess. Unfortunately, no police issue handcuffs are the right size, shape or material to arrest fires so they always manage to get away with it. You might also wish to blame the marble boys or Mrs Entwhistle or any number of people but the fact of the matter is that there really is no point in blaming anyone. Although, it was obviously the marble boys.

When Stephen arrived he was greeted by a wreck of a place that didn't look at all like the house he used to live in. I suppose this is mainly due to the fact that the house he used to live in wasn't burnt down when he used to live in it. But it was also because this was his initial reaction and he would continue to use the phrase, 'I just didn't recognise the place', to get the most impact in any conversation about his former abode.

He decided to enter his home where his door would have been even though it no longer existed. The builders had told him that the building had been made safe for now and that he could go and recover anything he might find before the builders moved in properly to do what it is that builders do, which is building buildings.

The inside of Stephen's living room was completely charred, all up the walls and onto the ceiling where holes had been made by Malcolm as he worked his way onto the upper floor. The wallpaper was scorched and the floor looked as if it had melted due to the strange ripples etched across its surface.

He took a moment just standing in his living room taking everything in. He thought through all the great memories he had of sitting in there watching television and drinking tea and eating food and he was sad but for the wrong reasons.

There was yellow and black striped tape covering the bottom of the stairs in a cross indicating to Stephen and anyone else just as sensible that you shouldn't really go up to the second floor just in case you fall through and end up lying in front of some stairs with yellow and black striped tape in a cross covering them. If someone was to go up a second time then they would most certainly deserve to keep falling forever.

Stephen began looking through the lower floor of his house to see if anything fell under the umbrella of 'salvageable'. He began with the CDs and DVDs on his shelves. Most boxes were either melted or burned to a crisp but there were a decent amount of CDs that he was able to pry from the shelves as globular masses stuck together. It was not a similar situation with the bookshelf because all of the books that Stephen owned had been made using paper and, due to a point in history where they obviously had a completely irresolvable argument, fire and paper do not get along.

His TV was not salvageable, nor his DVD player. His CD-radio combo was a possibility so he grabbed that. A lot of his crockery and cutlery were fine but these hadn't overly concerned him so he left them there for now. Most of his furniture was pretty defunct, especially the table and chairs in the kitchen, which Stephen suddenly regretted choosing for the reason that, 'Wicker will be easy to get home though, won't it?' In a possibly related argument, wicker and fire do not get along that great either (see 'The Wicker Man' for further information).

And so he collected the remnants of his possessions and put them into a cardboard box that had been lying around (which is very odd, because fire and cardboard aren't exactly best friends either, Malcolm must have not seen it) and he meandered back to Wendy's house. Judging by the state his house was in, he knew that Wendy's would remain his home for quite a while.

'Get anything?' came the call from the kitchen as Stephen entered Wendy's home. It was a Thursday and Wendy had come home early from work because two managers that refused to speak to one another thought she was working all day with the manager that they had a 'no speaking' policy with. It was a cleverly constructed plan that worked most Thursdays. It was now dinnertime so Wendy and Stephen had decided to make dinner because the time when dinner is most aptly fitting is dinnertime. Wendy had made a start whilst Stephen had gone back to his house to find any salvageable possessions.

'Not really,' said Stephen as he walked in the kitchen door, 'Just some questionable CDs and a CD-radio combo'

'When you say questionable, do you mean their state or your taste in music?'

'Well, I meant their state but I suppose the other option is a matter of opinion.'

'Let's take a look here.' She put down the knife that she had been using to cut up carrots and grabbed the melted pile of plastic. 'Beatles. Good. Beach Boys. Yep. Bowie. Fine... These are all Bs.'

'It was the only part of my CD collection that wasn't charred. I'm just left with a load of 'B' CDs.'

'Oh. They were alphabetised. That's... fun.'

'Hey, if I wanted to listen to a CD, it was good to know where they were.'

'This Björk one is still in the packaging.'

'Okay. Fine. I just preferred them organised.' The fact that she had caught him seemed to amuse her.

'Let's listen to Sergeant Pepper's,' she said. She struggled to prise open the melted plastic that held the CD case closed. Eventually it gave way with a satisfying crack, forcing Wendy to jump backwards slightly. She plugged in Stephen's CD player that he had salvaged from his burnt down home and they waited in silence as she put the CD on, unsure of whether the music would play. But it suddenly filled the little kitchen and Wendy began to dance while she chopped more carrots. Stephen awkwardly joined in, not feeling entirely comfortable with the whole dancing thing. At least he could disguise it with food preparation.

This might seem like the beginning of a romance. But don't worry, it's not as boring and predictable as all that. I know that might disappoint some people. But that's not what happened. Wendy was just helping Stephen through a bit of a tough time and she also really liked The Beatles.

The two dancers eventually sat down to dinner. The whole process had actually taken a little longer because of all the dancing but it was altogether more fun as well. The CD was singing 'When I'm Sixty-Four' as the two began munching on their meals. Just at the moment that Stephen placed some chicken in his mouth, the CD sang out 'Will you still feed me?' They both shared a chuckle at this rather unexciting coincidence and continued with the rest of their meal.

It was getting very late before they realised they had been happily chatting in the kitchen for the entire evening and that the 'repeat' button had started to grow what looked like a question mark after the word 'repeat'. The night occurred as normal in that the sun went down and the moon became more apparent. This was Stephen and Wendy's cue to discuss cleaning up the kitchen, conclude that it could wait until the morning and go to bed.

Stephen was filled with a strange excitement as he lay thinking in bed. The reason he was so excited was because tomorrow brought the promise of meeting those who had seen one of his posters and decided they were in the same position as him. He thought of all the people that he'd meet who feel lost or confused and how they would be able to discuss all of the things that have been troubling him. He felt the need to hear his thoughts articulated by someone else. He lay and simply thought for a while and these thoughts slowly blended with the beginnings of a dream. Stephen lay with his eyes closed in the accustomed way of sleeping that he had grown used to.

Inside his head there were many thoughts swilling around his synapses. There was one where he was singing Beatles songs to a room full of anthropomorphised goats. There was another where he discovered that all of his body parts were locked away in various filing cabinets across Asia. Just as he was about to try and locate his body parts at the same time as wondering how he would get anywhere without a body, he found he was sitting by a fire in the snowy climes of a distant land witnessing a ritual. People were handing around a cup which they would take from the person to their left, raise to their mouths, swill the contents and spit back in again. They would then pass it on to the next in the circle. Stephen's dream-self thought he was an onlooker until he suddenly realised that he was next in the circle. He gazed in a dreamy haze at the long-haired man that was offering up the cup of liquid which he had very recently swilled through the inner recesses of his mouth.

'Why are we doing this?' Stephen heard himself say, although he knew that he was speaking another language to this man. The man replied in the same language but Stephen's dream-self understood every word.

'To please the mighty Bango.'

'Oh,' said Stephen's dream-self and then he thought that this was all a bit silly.

An Intermission

I t has come to my attention as narrator of this tale that parts of it are much too light-hearted and whimsical. If anything, it's all becoming a little too easy. There are some that say stories should challenge people but these are exactly the sort of people that enjoy challenges as opposed to, say, ice-cream. But since this is all so very important (and I cannot stress enough how important all of this is) and being, as I am, a very serious narrator, I shall draw your attention to something that will, no doubt, whet your appetite for what is to come later in our story.

While researching the events that occurred to Stephen Moore, I discovered a very interesting piece of literature that recalls some words spoken by Stephen at a very crucial moment in his life. The reason I think they are interesting is the significance they hold rather than because they're useful. In fact, I think there is a direct correlation between how significant they are and how useful they aren't. And, I suppose, I described them as being spoken at a very crucial moment in Stephen's life because he didn't really have very much life left at the time he said them. It seems that it wasn't quite as crucial as one would think because he had the time to spin a little yarn. This little yarn doesn't make very much sense unless you've already sneaked a little look at the end of the book. If there is still some confusion about the correct way to read a book then please do refer to Chapter 1. For those of you who are clear about the whole reading thing then please allow me to make everything else a little less clear:

Ouch! That really hurts. It feels like a constant, piercing ache that will never cease. It is throbbing with my every heartbeat. But I shouldn't be here too long and when I go back to that place again I know the pain will disappear as if it were never there, along with the concept of pain itself.

I've sat there for quite a while on my little spot. It's probably been somewhere between two hours and seven thousand years. I've lost count because I don't feel the need to count. If you never want something to end and you know inside yourself that it never will then counting becomes obsolete. I do not wish to attempt to measure incomparable happiness. For one, it distracts us from the thing itself by getting bogged down in figures and for another it is so absolute that there would be no use in even trying. Here it was about a minute but, in a place where counting is obsolete, time becomes irrelevant and so barely exists at all.

It is lovely there, though. That is the only word I can think of to describe the place. It is just plain lovely. And hot. Unless you prefer it quite cool because it is that as well. And it is everything in between. I can just sit and let the waves crash onto the shore and, as they smoothly roll back out to sea, I can watch as they take with them my fears and anxieties. Each new wave only replenishes me with new forms of hope and happiness. It really is very lovely.

As I sit, thoughts enter my head but they are not the old, fuzzy thoughts that they used to be, the thoughts that would linger and disappear as soon as I went near them. The old, taunting thoughts that were full of promise but would scurry silently into the abyss only to return years later, disguised and just out of reach. These new thoughts are different. They are the clearest and most profound thoughts I have ever experienced, and they just sit there in my head. They do not run away as I try to explore them. They just sit boldly, happily and they willingly make everything clear.

I have sat a while on my little spot. I simply sit and think and it is enough. I have everything I have ever wanted and some other stuff I didn't even know that I wanted and all of these things are swimming around inside my head, making this whole experience very, very lovely.

I am alone now, but I am not lonely. I can only vaguely recall what loneliness is. For a while I thought I was entirely alone. One day this proved to be false but it also became true later on in the day.

It was one particular anonymous time-span between my usual three extended moments of pondering and an extended moment and a half of musing that a rustling noise disturbed my train of thought. I remember it vividly because it just so happened that this particular train of thought was about trains.

The rustle had arrived over my left shoulder. I calmly turned around to see what was there. It was a pair of dark eyes surrounded by tall grass. They were a little way off from me as I was near the shore but, on further investigation, I could see the hint of a beard protruding through the grass that told me it was a man that had, at the very least, reached puberty. The eyes were far off but, just when I thought that I would be able to place suspicion in them, they only exuded openness. Suddenly, a body appeared from out of the grass. It was connected to the eyes and the beard in the usual locations and it bounded clumsily towards me. He wore nothing at all. It was a man, but not quite. It was the essence of a man. It was a man without cares and with only satisfied dreams.

'You have come!' he screamed with exuberance as he grew closer to me. I stood up, feeling no threat, not entirely understanding what threat was, and was greeted by his embrace.

'Welcome! Welcome!' he sang. He let go of the embrace and began walking back towards the grass and he put his hand on my shoulder and lightly encouraged me to walk with him. 'It seems that your journey has just begun while mine is coming to a close.' These words puzzled me. He didn't seem old. If I were to equate him to Earth years I would say perhaps forty-five, although it *seems age is a distant memory here. There was something familiar in his eyes, though. Something boundless.*

It was then that we passed through the grass, past the wooded glade and found ourselves at the most beautiful oasis. Birds cackled and dipped their wings in the water as they glided across its surface. The faint trickle of a stream entering the pool was heard. The water was deep but clear. I could see large, colourful fish swimming along the bottom. Plants of every variety encased the pool save for the one entrance we had used. It was solitude.

'Am I to take it that your name is Stephen?' said the man. I was not afraid that he was aware of this; I already knew he was. As he asked, there was that familiarity in his eyes once more. I simply nodded.

'In that case, you bring with you my second death.' I was unfeeling as he said these words. I felt no guilt. I knew this was the way it was meant to be and so did he. He was not angry or distressed, merely accepting. 'The time has come,' he said, 'I know that you know what you must do. I need say no more on that subject.' He suddenly fell backwards onto the sand that surrounded the lake but he did so gracefully as if choreographed. And he beckoned me closer to his chosen spot and he began to tell me things, wondrous things, baffling things and slowly he slipped away.

And as he spoke, I took in every word. Nothing was lost to the sky. It was recorded and stored in my mind exactly as spoken. I heard it echo and adhere to the inside of my skull.

And that is why I have briefly come back from The Island. I was sitting alone and suddenly the clearest thought entered my mind. It was somehow clearer than all of the other clear thoughts I have experienced on my little spot. It was a thought that told me something that I had always known but had not realised until that moment. I realised my duty. And my duty is this: it is to spread the tale of Love, Peace, Happiness and Goldfish to humanity. These words were not written by me. Nor were they written by the bearded man. They were written through both of us. And I am here to retell the words he uttered on his chosen spot. These words are as old as time itself yet as young as an unborn child. They proudly exist. But they have not been written yet. They are ubiquitous. I hope you may find solace in their thoroughly profound meaning and any further questions should be addressed to The Island.

Love, Peace, Happiness and Goldfish

Then everything was Golden.

*And Nature and I turned to one another and pointed
to the sky;
For oranges are not a paradox nor lemons.*

*But everyone moaned at the prospect and the prospect
felt offended and appalled and basket.
And they dipped their toe in the fountain of eternal youth
for fear of getting wet.*

*Is this a Bench I see before me?
A place which I once loved more than any other.*

*May it remain standing, proud through the trial of time.
And the sounds and the sights and the tastes and the smells
and the feelings made people say, 'five is too many,' and
the dogs said, 'woof'.*

*And a woman's voice sang through the wind from the
South.
'Don't talk to me that way, young man; use your mouth.'*

And he began to tell me a tale.
It was about him telling his tale.
It told of his life and his death yet to come and he truly
told it so well.
He told me of everything that had ever occurred and it
took him a lifetime to tell.

But everyone shuddered at the idea and the idea shuddered
back and everyone wondered why the world shook.
There is no sense in counting; counting is only for those
with something to fear or something to cook.

The water cascaded or, rather, it fell so a man said, 'I'll
call that a waterfall'.
Then a woman said, 'I thought of it first,' and she held
up her barrel to catch it all.
And they danced in the joy of the springtime and thought
of Love and Peace and Happiness and Goldfish and the
bottom of the ocean and corkscrews and waving and paper
and leaves and Autumn that follows Spring.

'Millions of what?' said a small child. 'You can be a
millionaire after a million breaths and a million steps
and a million handshakes.'
And he shook his hand in the air in disgust and anger
and chocolate.

A smile flew across the sky, a mile high smile, and it grinned at everyone and everyone grimaced and went inside but their insides were gone.

And so the quest had begun. They were to find the Staircase. Everyone packed their lives into a hanky on a stick and their insignificance revealed itself.
But one became an expert, an expert in expertise, which made him an expert expert. This made him jump, for he was an expert in jumping.

'No, no, no, no, no' muttered a small, old woman, 'this isn't how it was meant to be.'
And so she walked on her feet instead.

A man that could only count to five missed out four and went straight to six. He cheered but no one heard and he calculated to cut his losses with a knife.
But he changed his mind and he held on. If he let go then everything was lost: his rope, his shoes, his stick and his hanky.
The tree trunk creaked and creaked and snapped and creaked a little bit more and then he fell, screaming, towards inevitability.
'Only God can save me now,' he cried and he moaned and he screamed and he groaned and he would've whimpered but he didn't have time because he hit the ground.

And they all thought of Love and Peace and Happiness and Goldfish.

A loud explosion made them run for their lives but their lives had run too fast.
And most people ducked but some goosed and they all wistfully looked into the future to see what it held in its Platinum hands.

A young woman turned to the crowd that surrounded
To see her express what had made her dumbfounded
'Rhyme' rhymes with itself. Is that a coincidence?'
'Don't talk rubbish!' they screamed with insistence.

One man found a diamond and said, 'it's mine.' So he opened a mine to find more and they glistened in the moonlight as the rain dropped onto their pure surface. But the mine collapsed.
The man is presumed dead, which is the 'Stage Right' before definitely dead.

*They fought for their rights and their wrongs and their
dignity and hypocrisy and the voice bellowed from behind
The mountains,
'You have no idea about the laws of the oceans or the
mighty hand that guides you there'.
They replied with something quite witty but it's hard to
remember exactly.
Nobody wanted to say what they all thought was true
and their false smiles wore thin in the sleet, 'my feet, they
are weary and my hands cannot hold. My teeth feel like
ice-cubes cracking my gums.'*

*But nothing could stop this incredible beast that tore
up what stood in its way until a small girl with eyes the
size of rubies shone them into its face. And his grinding
teeth stopped and he looked down in confused awe for,
he thought to himself, he had never seen eyes quite like
that before.*

*And the screams shattered glass on the sides of the streets
as the people all stared into space.
'From where do we come? And why are we here? And
what's this strange mark on my face?'
Their first two were answered with bellowing beauty but
the last one was too tricky to the taste.
And as everyone shouted in realisation, they thought of
their luck and their fortune and fate.*

And, after it all, a man sang from a rooftop and it was all made clear.
'The reason we are here, is to find the reason we are here.
Our work here is done,' he said.

And, as the bearded man slid into his second death, he glared with importance as he said,

'One must respect the Staircase and learn to wait,
For one could meet a most unhealthy fate.'

And their thoughts turned once again to Love, Peace, Happiness and Goldfish.

Then everything was silent.

For silence is golden.

And all of the colours joined their fingerless hands to create an
Enigma
Of endless sorts.

Stephen Moore at The Bench

19th January 2009

(Apparently)

Well, that's quite enough of that. I'm hoping this has left you in somewhat of a state of curiosity. All of that nonsense will contribute to the general importance of this book in due time, I hope. I just feel as though a little bewilderment will keep you here so that you can read everything you need to read. I'm very keen to tell you what happened to Stephen but as the old saying goes, 'A little bit of bewilderment, be it as little as an ant or something more akin to a stick insect or grasshopper, can certainly add a little bit of flavour to a story, that is, a flavour in the sense of an element of interest as opposed to an actual flavour you can taste. Please don't try and eat the story. No, stop that.' It is one of my favourite sayings.

Chapter 7

'Don't talk to me that way, young man; use your mouth'

Stephen awoke in Wendy's spare room. He was quite used to being there now so it didn't shock him this time. He had forgotten all of the dreams he had had during the night as usual. He clambered out of bed and headed towards the kitchen for some breakfast.

His day occurred to a sufficient level of boring.

The time of the meeting finally came and Stephen wandered quite joyfully around to the local community centre, quietly expecting a small mob. He was not greeted by such a sight. Nothing close. There was a single, small, stocky man waiting patiently outside the main entrance, looking somewhat lost. He held an unlit cigarette in his mouth and he was patting around his clothes, clearly searching for something to light it with. He perked up as he saw Stephen crossing the road towards the entrance of the building. The man had the appearance of an excitable bulldog.

'Are you here for the meeting?' he said, his eyes looking hopeful through his thick glasses.

'Actually, I'm the one organising it. Is there anyone else around?'

'No. Just me for the moment. I didn't want to wait inside alone.'

'So you thought you'd wait outside alone?'

'Well, yeah, that and I wanted a ciggie. You haven't got a match or a lighter on you, by any chance?'

Stephen patted down all of his clothes even though he knew for certain that he didn't have a lighter or a match or anything resembling them.

'Afraid not. I don't smoke.'

'Clever man!' he said as he removed the cigarette and placed it back in his pocket. 'I'm trying to cut down, myself. Anyway, where are my manners? I'm Brian.' He offered out his hand. Stephen took the hand and shook it and became more baffled with each added second that the man seemed to hold on and grip his hand tighter. It was certainly not common handshaking etiquette.

'I'm Stephen. Nice to meet you,' he lied.

'Very nice to meet you, Stephen. Shall we head in?' he said as he signalled over his shoulder with his spare thumb, still not letting go of Stephen's hand.

'Yes. I suppose we better had,' replied Stephen slowly, trying to remove his hand at the same pace as his voice.

They both entered into the rusty corridor of the community centre's main entrance. Even when they found the light-switch it didn't get that much lighter. This was because the light was broken. Luckily the waning dusk from outside was providing just about enough light for them to find their way to the main hall. As they entered, Stephen groped his way along a wall, finding various uninviting textures until he located something akin to a light-switch. He pressed it and the hall flickered into view. It was a reasonably large hall, which became emphasised by the fact that there were currently only two people in it. It had an old, wooden stage at its far end and fading wooden floorboards in an indistinguishable pattern streaming across the floor. Several tables and chairs were stacked up on either side of it and it carried the same heavy, musky smell of the corridor, tinged with the strange freshness of cleaning products that are bought in bulk.

Stephen and Brian decided it best to gather a table and a few chairs for the meeting. Then it was just a case of waiting for all the others to arrive. As it turned out, no one else came that first week.

'Two isn't bad,' thought Stephen in his mind and then his mind made his mouth say, 'I'm sure there'll be more next week.'
'Yeah, I'm sure there will be,' said Brian.

But then Stephen thought further. 'Two isn't bad' is quite inaccurate because he was guaranteed so, really, there was only one.

The meeting was a reasonable level of difficult as it almost always is with two people who don't know each other. That is unless you're some kind of social anomaly that is comfortable enough to be entirely yourself within the first few minutes of a conversation with a person you do not know. So, of course, both Stephen and Brian were exceptionally nice as they began their conversation.

'So,' attempted Stephen, 'do you live near here?'

'Yes. That's how I saw your poster.'

'Of course,' said Stephen, remembering suddenly why there's very rarely any point in starting a conversation. 'Anywhere specific?'

'What? Where I saw your poster?'

'Yes. Okay,' said Stephen. He had, of course, meant 'Anywhere specific where you live?' which, besides being an awfully constructed sentence, was not worth correcting Brian over. If the poster question was easier to get a conversation going then Stephen felt it best to go with that one.

'I saw it in the park. It was on a tree.'

'Oh, there we are then,' said Stephen and then he started to feel the silence again. He had to do something quick. 'I like trees,' was the best he came up with.

'Do you?' said Brian

'Yes,' said Stephen.

There was a prolonged silence again, but Stephen suddenly leapt into action.

'So, what do you want from these meetings, Brian?' Brian paused for a moment. He seemed shocked by Stephen's sudden formality but he went along with it anyway.

'That's a good question, Stephen. I suppose,' he paused for a moment and then the moment became a bit longer and then it was ridiculously long for a person to be thinking over anything but eventually he began talking again. 'I want some kind of direction. Perhaps some kind of guidance. Perhaps a few answers to some deep questions. Just this and that, really.'

'Not a lot, then,' thought Stephen but he found himself instead saying something vague and meaningless:

'Well, we'll see what we can do.' Suddenly and without warning from any part of his brain he had become some kind of organisation. He had used 'we' twice in a sentence when the only remotely truthful word could be 'I'. But it was too late. That sentence had just made Brian far too happy. Stephen began again, trying to ignore Brian's sudden happiness as well as trying to find out more about Brian's recent musings.

'Okay. Well what do you mean by direction?'

'Oh, just where I'm going in life.'

'Right,' said Stephen, remembering again why there's often no point in conversation. Not in a spiteful way. He knew he could be as irritating as anyone, which was why he didn't like to force himself into situations where someone else could come to the same conclusion about him. It just so happened that Brian seemed to be fulfilling that particular role in this conversation. It was the process of conversation more generally that he didn't enjoy and he remembered it more often when he talked to people. This obvious correlation had to be ignored briefly. 'Let's start slowly,' began Stephen, 'Shall I assume you were of Christian faith?'

'That is correct.'

'And what changed things?'

'Well, I started having doubts when I thought it through properly.'

'How do you mean?' asked Stephen.

'Well, it's a bit far-fetched, isn't it?' said Brian.

'Yes, well, I suppose it is.' and they both laughed for twenty seconds or so.

'But that doesn't make it all alright,' said Brian, interrupting the laughter with an unfortunate air of seriousness, 'because what should I do now?' And he stopped in a kind of dramatic pause that I will illustrate with a small gap below.

'Who am I?'

'What do you mean by, "who am I"? You're Brian. You're you. You're not defined by what you believe in, are you?'

'I'm not sure. I know you're right but I suppose I used to be.'

Stephen considered this. For the first time in the conversation he knew exactly what Brian meant. This was something he had struggled with since his faith left him on the evening of the fire but he resolved that he should take on the air of someone that was trying to help. As he spoke he was obviously asking these questions to Brian but in a less obvious way he was asking these questions to himself.

'Well what else drives and defines you?'

'Well...' Brian was clearly struggling. Stephen once again understood. He knew how hard this was. But he rephrased the question to try again.

'Is there anything else you do? Anything else you love?'

'I've always loved writing,' returned Brian cheerily. In contrast to most people who will reluctantly admit to such things in a quiet and reserved manner, Brian seemed suddenly very keen to talk about this subject. 'You know, bits here and there, poems, short stories. I'd love to get around to writing something meaty and substantial. I just need some kind of drive to do it.'

'I'm sure you can do it, Brian. There's nothing stopping you. You don't need all the other stuff. This can be what defines you.' This set off a curious glint in Brian's eye. Stephen had said something which seemed to greatly please him. He seemed to be drifting off on several trains of thought at once before he stopped himself and resumed the conversation.

'Well what about you, Stephen? What happened to you?'

'My house burnt down. And I suppose it was a sort of culmination of events.'

'Oh, I'm sorry, that's awful. Was it a last straw scenario?'

'Yeah, it was. It was a kind of first and last straw and everything in between scenario in one evening.' Stephen felt good to finally be talking about this but he was also keen to keep things going, to try and look to the future. He brought the conversation back.

'Do you ever wish you could forget about all of this and just go back to the way it was? To go back to a time when you had faith?'

'Oh, all the time,' said Brian. 'That's part of why I'm here. Part of me wishes I'd never resolved everything in my head the way I did. I just wish I had that feeling in my life still.'

They talked for a little longer, some unimportant things were said, some important things that I can't remember were said and, after having sat in the old hall for about half an hour with no one else having arrived, they decided it was best to leave.

'We'll put more posters up and see if we can get more along next week,' said Stephen.

'Okay. That was a good meeting,' said Brian. 'Fancy going down the pub for a pint?'

In Stephen's head he screamed out 'WHAT?' very loudly and he thought, 'but we just had a meeting. What's the point in having a meeting and then going somewhere else to have a meeting?' and even though his mind was saying this, he kindly said,

'Actually, Brian, I'm a bit tired and I'm probably just going to head back. Thanks anyway, though. I'll see you next week.'

'Right-o' said Brian, a little archaically, 'See you next week.'

They both wandered out of the hall. They entered what was now a very dark corridor, much darker than on their arrival due to the habit that the night has of doing that to things. They felt their way down to the main entrance. The darkness was hugging them as they slid their hands along the walls to make sure they got to a door. They headed out in search of a street lamp to guide them on their way home.

Stephen remained reasonably confident that next week's meeting would prove to be a better one. He also continued to harbour some curiosity for Brian's strangely haunting look after Stephen encouraged him to get back to his writing. There was something about it that did not sit well with Stephen. However, it wasn't enough to overly worry him so instead of going through the difficult task of worrying about things, Stephen opted for not worrying in the slightest and he continued his evening in a normal fashion and eventually went to bed.

Chapter 8

Straight To Six

I t was more out of habit than anything else. He just meandered in and then realised the situation quite suddenly. What I mean to say is, he was not an active participant in that morning's events. All of these sentences seem like I'm trying to make some kind of an excuse for Stephen's actions. That's because I am. It was a Sunday morning and Stephen found himself sitting in a church.

He was looking around and, for the first time in such a location, feeling a little out of place. He was a person that felt a little out of place in most situations but never here. I only wish you could have seen him but, unfortunately, this whole thing wasn't being filmed so these words will have to suffice. I have to tell you somehow and this all very important.

He sat next to Mrs Peterson. Mrs Peterson seemed like she was a kind and gentle old woman but this was not the case. She did a strange thing that people sometimes do where they force you to join in a conversation by asking a strange question that could normally only have cropped up halfway through a conversation. Those words I just wrote are somewhat confusing so perhaps I will show you because she did this very thing during the next couple of minutes which is convenient. Mrs Peterson swiftly turned away from Mrs Neil and confronted Stephen with a very strange form of greeting:

'Well, it's just against God's Nature, isn't it?' This vague and odd question obviously forced Stephen into a conversational corner. He had only one thing that he could possibly say and so he did:

'I'm sorry, what is?'

'The gays, dear,' said Mrs Peterson, 'Against God, isn't it?' Stephen, once again, had been forced into a conversational corner. Debates are very rare in churches. There's a lot of nodding but very little debate and so Stephen was forced to simply say,

'Yes. Yes, I suppose it is.' This made Mrs Peterson very happy indeed. She nodded at Stephen's forced agreement and, before she could add to the less than intelligent discussion, the vicar at the front began speaking.

'Good morning,' he said, 'and what a glorious morning it is, too. We thank the Lord for this glorious morning he has delivered to us. In addition,' said the vicar, seeming worried that the good Lord may have lost interest as most people do with conversations about weather, 'we'd like to thank him for the good health of the people here before us, especially as the winter months are drawing in.'

Things seemed to go on like this, with the vicar saying something about the weather or reading from the Bible.

Stephen sang along perfectly nicely with the hymns and he looked down properly when it was time to pray. His mind was partially struggling with some parts of the service but the vicar interrupted his thoughts by introducing a small passage from the Bible.

'Now, we can have interpretations and we can have difficult issues raised and while things get analysed and evaluated and even ridiculed, we can take comfort in parts of the Bible that are undiluted and loving truths. This is a simple line I often turn to that sums up perfectly why each and every one of you is here: "God is love, and he who abides in love abides in God, and God abides in him."' The vicar looked up from his Bible, saw all of the faces listening to him and began to explain the significance of this reading, 'because God loves every one of us. He loves all the people gathered in this room. Even if you stray, he'll help to guide you back. And he loves your friends and relatives, even those that have strayed so far as to sin. Because we're all sinners here, aren't we? But Jesus died for our sins, he died to cleanse us, he died to give us hope so that we may thrive off God's eternal forgiveness and so that we may find our way to heaven one day.' There was a small silence before the vicar spoke again. But within this silence Stephen digested all that was just said. His mind moved through a few thought processes and, suddenly and very loudly, inside his head, he thought:

'This is horrible.'

Without anything that vaguely resembled an excuse to leave, Stephen stood around the empty teacups and the paper plates with biscuits covered in cling film and waited around to see who would approach him first.

It was Mrs Watson, who really was a kindly old woman (much more so than the façade of kindly that Mrs Peterson portrays), who was the first to see him standing alone.

'Have you got yourself a cup of tea, Stephen?' she said.

'No, I was just about to pour one. Would you like one?' he offered.

Stephen turned to the table and poured two cups of tea from the big pot that had been made up. He removed the cling film from the biscuit plate and offered them to Mrs Watson. She took a custard cream and thanked him. He turned back and gave her the tea he'd just made.

'So...' he offered.

'Nice service, wasn't it, dear?'

'Um... yeah, lovely.' He tried to disguise his indifference and partial horror but he felt quite comfortable with Mrs Watson. She was an old lady with a good sense of humour and he'd always found her easy to talk to. He took this moment, far enough away from everyone else, to try and find out about her faith and its stability; to try and find some consolation in what he was doing. More than anything, he was doing this to feel less guilty than he currently did.

'Mrs Watson?'

'Oh, dear, you know by now that you can call me Maggie.'

'Sorry, of course, Maggie?' he asked as he took a bite from a digestive biscuit that he'd just softened in his tea.

'Yes.'

'You've been a Christian, I take it, your whole life?'

'That's correct, yes.'

'Have you ever found…? I mean to say, have you ever been in the situation where…?' He was really struggling. He didn't know how he was going to phrase this.

'Come on, dear. Out with it. You know you can ask me.'

'Um… have you ever had your faith tested?' He felt better immediately after asking it. The ball of elastic bands that had been contracting in his stomach suddenly released themselves (see in dictionary: metaphor), and he began to smile. He looked at the old woman's face as she looked away from him for the answer. She seemed to be looking deep into her memory recesses. She was searching hard for the profound answer that Stephen wanted. This was an old woman but you could tell from her eyes that, as a youngster, she used to be fun and know happiness. She was just the sort of person Stephen wanted to be talking to right now. He felt her answer coming back and he was excited for it. She slowly turned back to him, looked him in the eye and said,

'No.'

There was a very brief silence as Stephen struggled to hold back his disappointed shock but he moved on.

'Oh. No, of course not. Silly stuff,' he said.

'I find that people who, "have their faith tested," or whatever that modern and ridiculous term is, are just making excuses for the fact that they just can't be bothered to get out of bed on a Sunday. Of course everyone believes in God, how could they not? He's just so, well, brilliant!' She concluded this by lifting her free arm and her voice at the same time. Stephen agreed.

Chapter 9 begins almost exactly from where Chapter 8 finishes. This suggests that there probably wasn't any point in a chapter break but I'm in charge around here.

Chapter 9

Only A Little Further

After the accidental church visit Stephen arrived home to Wendy sitting on the sofa reading a book. She didn't look up from the book, however, as she greeted his arrival in the living room.

'Hello, Stephen,' she said. 'Good service?'

'What?' he said, quite distantly. 'Oh. Yeah. Nice.'

'That's nice.'

'How did you know I'd gone?'

'Just figured it out,' she returned. She stopped reading mid-word, put her bookmark between the pages she was on and closed and lowered the book to the coffee table that didn't have any coffee on it. She looked up at him. 'So, what are your plans for the rest of the day? Fancy going for a walk?'

'Yeah. That might be nice.'

Stephen and Wendy found themselves going for a nice, leisurely walk around the park. Both were very quiet to begin with, just taking in the trees and the birds singing and the storm cloud coming over the horizon.

'So, did your meeting go well the other day?' asked Wendy, breaking the silence, not in a violent manner, you understand.

'Yes. Well, no, actually.'

'Oh?'

'Well, there was only one person there. A guy named Brian. A bit odd but I'm sure he means well. We had a few small discussions but that was it really.'

'What were you hoping for?'

'To be honest, I don't have a clue. I've always had something or, rather, someone watching over me. I've thought about some things that Brian was talking about and I can see what he means now. He was talking about how he used to have a 'direction'. I've always had a direction. How do you cope?' asked Stephen.

'Well, very easily if I was to be perfectly honest. I've never really believed in anything supernatural and I just made the logical step. Once I'd got through the stage of finding out about the Tooth Fairy, the Easter Bunny and, of course, Father Christmas, I just went one step further. What made sense when I was a child didn't when I had grown up a bit.'

'I envy you, Wendy. Even though I feel like it's making sense suddenly, there's still a niggle. I need my direction.'

'Can't you make it yourself? Direction is a very vague word indeed, Stephen. It sounds like an excuse wrapped up neatly in a three-syllable word.'

'Well, that's exactly it. Some people would argue that it's almost four syllables, not exactly, but almost, as though we're not looking at it properly.'

'That's all very deep and thoughtful and the like, Stephen, but can I ask you something?'

'Yes, of course.'

'What the hell are you talking about?' And after a brief pause they both laughed haughtily for longer than the normal designated and acceptable laughing time. Especially considering the fact that what was said wasn't particularly funny. At times Stephen couldn't walk anymore and was forced to bend and lift himself up weirdly as his stomach tensed too much for him to cope with. They concluded that they should go over and sit on the bench nearest to them.

As they lowered themselves onto the bench the last portions of laughter escaped them slowly. It was the kind of laughing that teases you, where it almost ends but then a strange inward breath can throw you off and get you going again but it gradually tittered away with a sigh.

Again, non-violently, Stephen broke the silence.

'You're right, though,' he said and suddenly an air of seriousness had returned but it was nothing that Wendy couldn't handle.

'I'm always right, Stephen,' she joked.

'No, I know,' he returned, 'but even more so than normal.'

'I see.'

'I mean...' He paused and then he slowly released a titter which became a chuckle which became a chortle which turned, one way or another, into a guffaw and he did that eternally amusing thing where someone struggles desperately to say something but cannot control the laughter that is trying to escape their mouths at the same time. This seems to be even funnier when the thing they're trying to say is a kind of conclusive or universal thought that sums everything up nicely. I will show you what I mean. Stephen's guffaw was becoming louder and he began to wipe a tear from his face as he concluded with great effort, 'What was I up to?' and, once again, despite nothing overly funny occurring, the laughter began to rise.

If you're getting bored with all of this laughter and happiness (which, frankly, I am) then I would suggest perhaps watching a depressing film but if you're comfortable with all of this sickening happiness then do read on. If you are of the persuasion that you feel that you can put up with it for a bit longer as long as it ends soon then you can read on in the comfort that I promise you it will.

'Oh it's good to laugh again,' said Stephen, 'I can't remember the last time I had a good and proper laugh.'

And a little while later, with several teasing moments where one would think it had ended but it started up again, the laughter entirely faded away.

'So, when's your next meeting?'

'Friday. I hope there are more people than last time. If it's just Brian and me again I think I'd struggle for another hour and to come up with a new excuse to get away from the pub.'

'I'm sure there'll be more people. Do you know what you're going to talk about or try and get done?'

'No.' The reason that Stephen said this is because he didn't and the reason I'm ending the chapter here is because Chapter 10 is going to be almost as good as Chapter 8 and I wouldn't want to taint it with all of the pointless laughter that has become associated with Chapter 9.

Chapter 10

The Tree Trunk Creaked

It is largely unimportant what Stephen's job was. This is not because I don't know what his job was; it's just that it was largely unimportant. Vastly unimportant. In the grand scheme of things, in relation to the Universe, it's hard to pick any job of importance but Stephen's really was quite dull. At points he would forget what it was and then he would remember and then he would lightly sob. On that Monday that followed the Sunday, as it so cheekily tends to do, he decided to go into work for the first time in a couple of weeks.

He had had to buy a new suit for work since his old ones had recently burnt down in a fire (see Chapter 1). He took his new suit out of his cupboard (the cupboard that had become his in Wendy's house) and put it onto his freshly-showered self. He then left, doing the strangely fashionable thing that some people tend to do which is walking out of the house with a piece of toast in their mouth. It is a suggestion of, 'I'm so busy that I don't have time for simple and essential animalistic functions such as consuming food to survive.' Admittedly, they are very busy indeed and this isn't their fault. But now is not the time for blame. But if I was to blame anyone it would probably be the person that invented money. Then again, money is just an easy extension of the old system of bartering so it would be unfair to blame the inventor of money as this was a good decision on the whole. But, if we were to take trading back further, maybe it would be fair to blame whoever came up with the theory of deciding something is someone's, rather than something just being something and someone just being someone. I'm getting a bit out of my depth here. I think I'll just leave that there and begin another paragraph.

Stephen walked with his suit on top of his skin towards his car and drove towards his office. It became reasonably apparent when he got into the office that most (if not all) the people at his office were quite unaware of his recent absence or the fiery reason for it. This didn't bother Stephen overly. Upon arrival, he sat down in his swivel chair and swivelled it a few times, which seems only fair. These swivels began in small motions but in the end he gave in and went for the full three hundred and sixty degree swivel. However, he only got half-way around because he saw a very sulky-looking Sulky Barry wandering over to his desk.

'Morning, Barry. How's it going?' he asked, careful not to suggest he'd noticed that Barry was looking particularly sulky today. He had a tendency to sulk quite a lot and it was best not to draw attention to it because you might just have to hear why he was sulking. However, as Stephen found out that morning, the reason that he was sulking today was a little worse than normal and he didn't even have to ask to receive the answer.

'I'm alright, y'know. I'm coping. It's just, well; I thought I'd tell you before you heard it from someone else.'

'What is it, Barry?'

'Well, my mum died over the weekend.'

'Oh God, I'm so sorry, mate. That's terrible. I'm so sorry.' Stephen wasn't entirely sure what he was sorry for. As far as he knew, he had had nothing to do with Barry's mother's death. He thought back on his week and concluded that he could categorically say that he had had nothing directly to do with the death of anyone. Still, it's best not to retract a 'sorry' in most situations and certainly not this one. It's just a little rude.

'Oh, that's okay. I've sort of come to terms with it now.' Stephen knew he should say something else. He wasn't sure what, though. He'd heard people use the 'how did it happen?' one before but he always felt that was a bit much. What if it was, 'really horribly. She slipped onto some barbed wire' or something equally graphic. Probably best not to drag something like that up. Rather strangely and without any warning from his brain, his mouth said,

'How old did she make it to?' The reason this struck both men involved in this conversation as a little odd was because the wording of the question made life seem like some sort of competition.

'Ninety-Six' said Barry, relatively slowly and somewhat bemused.

'Oh,' said Stephen, trying his best to retain an acceptable level of enthusiasm. He offered something along the lines of, 'Well, she made it to a good old age,' which was a little obvious. As is often the case and as you will have gathered, silence tends to travel near Stephen and this moment was no exception. Stephen considered momentarily bringing up his burnt-down house but decided it was best not to try and trump Barry's dead mother.

It was Barry that spoke next with the beginnings of a request.

'There was just one thing,' said Barry, 'My mother was a very religious woman, you see. None of the rest of my family really is. And I know that you are. I was just wondering if you could think of a fitting reading or perhaps if you could write anything that she would appreciate or would have wanted at her funeral. You're most welcome along as well, Stephen.'

There was not the smallest ounce of Stephen's fibre that wanted to go to the funeral and so Stephen said what anyone would.

'I would be honoured to go along. And, certainly, I'll help out with a reading.'

'That's great, Stephen. She would be pleased. She would've wanted something from the Bible and I just wouldn't know where to start. I know you go to church so I just thought maybe that might be some help in finding something fitting.' Stephen, of course, hadn't admitted to anyone from work that he had lost his faith and this situation didn't make things any easier. He would have to remain in his religious closet for a little longer. 'What is it you'd say, Stephen? Oh yeah, at least she's in a better place now.'

'Yes. Yes. She will be.' And, for the first time in his life, Stephen didn't really mean that.

Chapter 11

They Glistened In The Moonlight

The next few days of work were a struggle. Stephen had to remain 'the religious guy' for a little longer so as not to offend or worry Sulky Barry. Barry had obtained his unfortunate nickname (which he was still entirely unaware of) when he sat alone for the whole evening at the office Christmas party complaining about the music, the drink availability, the company present, the location and more general complaints about his life, other people's lives and the state of the world. This had something to do with the fact that Barry had tipped over into the state of inebriation where one struggles to keep in what one really thinks about things. And, to be fair to Barry, it was a rubbish party and his life and the state of the world is not so great. But people can often be cruel and they chose to ignore the fact that they've been in the same situation and the even more obvious fact that the party was rubbish and decided to adopt a spiteful nickname instead. Still, he didn't mind, this was mainly because he didn't know about it. If he did know about it, he would mind. But, still, he didn't mind.

Stephen remained busy at his desk as Mr Lynam made his journey around to peruse his employees in his usual fashion. Mr Lynam was a man who, through his hobby of breeding and showing Rottweilers, had started to take on many of the features and mannerisms of the breed. Luckily, Stephen had figured out over the years that Mr Lynam was in a state that could be interpreted as 'happy' just as long as one's 'Out' tray was fuller than one's 'In' tray. He coincidentally figured out that the 'Out' tray was a fantastic place to store all of his empty envelopes and blank paper.

Once Mr Lynam had taken a strange sniff that managed to evoke both a disgruntled and satisfied opinion at the same time, he moved on from the sixth floor to the next one which caused a collective sigh from the workers.

Mr Lynam had a strange way of moving around the floors. The day of the month combined with which day of the week it fell on dictated in which order he would make his visits. He felt that this would help to surprise his employees and possibly catch one or two people off guard who had the ratio the wrong way around between their 'In' and 'Out' trays. Unfortunately for him, the employees worked together between the floors and had managed to collate the order he visited the floors and at what time he would arrive at each. Together, they had managed to crack his bizarre code. Mr Lynam felt that arriving at exact times within his secret order of floor visits would improve efficiency in the business but it actually meant that his employees had spent months using complex data entry programmes to outsmart him. As a consequence, they knew the exact time when they had to swap the signs of their 'In' and 'Out' trays and when it was safe for them to play office stationery bowling.

Thursday came around sooner than Stephen thought it would. This is very lucky for us because I don't have to bother you with any other unexciting details. Stephen left the office at exactly 5:02 in his off-grey suit. He left through the right-hand door of the double doors that lead out of his building. This is the one that isn't quite as creaky as the other one, although it also has a slight creak. As one leaves via the right door, however, one is more likely to step into the permanent puddle that is outside the office doors. But, as I say, I don't want to go into too much detail.

He travelled home in his car which has four wheels and up to six windows. He mainly used the road.

Stephen's Thursday night was filled with less excitement for the following day's meeting than it had done the week before. He went to the pub with Wendy and they discussed many topics. In the way that most conversations work, one led seamlessly into the other and they went as follows: Tea, Shot, Glass, House, Work, Force, Fields, Shall we go?

The two went to their beds. Stephen had several more dreams that he had forgotten by the morning. One involved him stamping up and down with his hands over his ears for ages while a bearded man stood in front of a chalk board and pointed at numbers. Another involved a talking cat that would insist on pronouncing Stephen with a 'v' instead of a 'ph' in the middle. Stephen could tell exactly when people were doing this and it really got to him. He awoke in the night strangling his pillow. He eventually got back to sleep.

The following evening, Stephen arrived at the community centre for his second attempt at a meeting. If I was to bore you with details then I'd tell you that he was wearing some stone-washed jeans and a red jumper but as I'm not boring you with details I will simply assure you that Stephen was fully clothed and not breaking any indecent exposure laws. As he rounded the corner, he saw a familiar figure across the street standing outside the centre but this time he wasn't alone. Brian was with two other people, talking about something or other, I think they were talking about other. This time he had remembered a light for his cigarette and so he was enjoying each puff in a break in the conversation and exhaling the smoke into the sky.

'Oh, there he is,' Stephen heard Brian say from a mild distance, pointing directly at him. The two people looked towards him looking distinctly nothing. Upon his arrival, Brian became somewhat over-excited. 'This is Stephen, he runs this thing.'

'Well, sort of,' said Stephen, 'I was hoping to get the ball rolling and then see how it goes.'

'Well, anyway. This is Stephen. Stephen, this is Flo and Matthew.' Flo was a short, dark-haired woman with eyes too big for her face. Not in a bad way, it's just that they were. Matthew had curly, dark hair and his eyes were normal size.

'Nice to meet you,' they all said in near enough unison.

'Shall we go in?' said Stephen. None of them answered verbally but they all began entering the building so Stephen guessed their answer.

After getting settled with a table and a few more chairs than last time, they began to discuss what they were actually going to do. Stephen had some ideas after last time.

'Brian, I hope you don't mind but your concerns from last time prompted some ideas for me, and I'd like to share that with the group.'

'Not a problem, Stevey-boy,' said Brian. Stephen wasn't sure whether he liked this premature familiarity. Actually, he was sure that he wasn't sure about it.

I should have mentioned earlier that Stephen had a bag containing a pad of paper and a pen but I only just remembered. He got these out of the bag after getting some enthused permission from Brian.

But first let's hear from Flo and Matthew. Coincidentally, this is what Stephen said.

'But first let's hear from Flo and Matthew. What brings you here?'

'Um. Well, shall I go first?' said Flo to Matthew. He gave his permission with a welcoming eyebrow raise, a hand gesture as if holding open a door and a strange mouse-like noise so Flo continued, 'Well, I've been questioning it all for years. I've never been what you might call devout but it suddenly all began to make sense, because, well, none of it made sense. So it was kind of a culmination and then one day I was just sitting there and thought, "No. No, that's enough." Nothing terribly interesting but that's why I'm here.'

'Okay. Great. Thanks, Flo. And Matthew?'

'Well. I'm not totally sure I should be here. I've sort of lost my faith but not totally. I just want to explore all the possibilities. I mean, I'm still going to church, I just want to look at it all and then decide.'

'Okay. Great. Thanks to you, too, Matthew. Okay then, let's get some of these ideas written down. I don't know if your concerns are the same as Brian's but he was worried about a lack of 'direction', as he called it, but more than this, it was a concern about not knowing what's right and wrong any more. Because the Bible had always told him what was right and wrong. I thought perhaps we could just write these down independently of a religion, just what we truly and rationally believe is right and wrong.'

'That sounds like a fantastic idea, Stevey-boy,' said Brian. Stephen paused for a moment and looked at Brian with only a small amount of contempt for his new nickname. But he made sure this contempt disappeared from his face and he said, 'Yes. Well, I thought so.' And they began.

Stephen's first word was less than lovely.

'Murder? I think we can agree that that's not so great. Let's have a vote, who would agree that murder's pretty nasty.' They all put their hands up. 'Okay. A good start. Let's write that down.'

And so the list was created. They collectively agreed that the following actions were bad:

Murder

Rape

Violence

Theft

They also agreed that hatred in its many forms were generally unwelcome which included: The hatred of another because of their race, religion, creed, country of origin, family's country of origin, sexual orientation, disability, accent, height, weight, age, political stance, ideological stance, standing stance as well as agreeing that we could work on our hatred for tea-slurpers, slow talkers, baffling talkers, wild talkers, annoying talkers, slow walkers, close sitters and those that are normally outcast as 'just plain weird'.

They collectively agreed that hatred even in its mildest form is generally not very nice.

But they felt that it was all getting a bit heavy, and perhaps they should look at some of the things they believe to be good:

Just generally being nice to each other. This includes: praising, consoling, helping, laughing, smiling and just being all-round, lovely people.

They continued to think about things they should generally encourage, but they agreed, rather, that this was kind of up to people. But they did write a small list of things they did not mind people doing.

Whatever they want as long as it doesn't harm others.

It was a very short list indeed.

'Fantastic,' said Stephen as he placed the list in the middle of the table for everyone to take a little look at. 'Well there we go, I think we've all agreed on things that are generally quite good and generally quite bad and maybe that gives us some solace that we can make our own mind up about these things.'

'I suppose it does, Stevey-boy.' Brian, who had been silent throughout the whole proceedings of the list writing, had now entered the conversation with little to no warning. 'I could take that and photocopy it and we could hand it to newcomers if you like.'

'Well. That's not really... We don't want to impose rules or anything... It's more about our own choices... Do you understand the last point on the...?' Stephen was struggling to finish each sentence because he was also struggling to keep back what he really wanted to say to Brian which was 'Stop being an idiot.' Instead, with a little persuasion, he watched Brian slowly fold up the paper and put it into his pocket as he talked about how good the photocopier people are across the road from him.

Stephen had to take a few moments to think about what had just happened and concluded that it would all probably be alright. It wasn't, of course.

'Um... well then. I suppose we should have a little bit more of a discussion. One of the things that was really bothering me was the fact that I wasn't really able to articulate how I actually feel now. Maybe together we can find something that we all share and make this whole process a little easier for one another. That's what this thing's about, after all.'

'As well as direction,' said Brian.

'Um... and that, too, if you want,' said Stephen, not entirely convinced that Brian was dealing all that well with this situation. His attempt at getting the conversation moving worked, however. They talked on the subject for well over the hour, agreeing with one another about how it feels, about how it's like a weight being lifted at the same time as losing a huge part of yourself. They only strayed slightly when they started talking about their favourite flavour of ice-cream. It was slightly related, however, and so they returned straight back into it before concluding that they would continue next week.

Stephen started feeling a lot better. He felt the most content he had since the night of the fire and this whole feeling better thing made him feel even better which, in turn, made him feel even better. This wonderful cycle went on for a little while until he was only slightly bored with feeling this good and he made the walk through the park and back to his temporary home.

Chapter 12

Dignity and Hypocrisy

Stephen found himself walking through the park with Elijah again on Sunday but he hadn't been to church beforehand. This walk wasn't just a time for walking, though. He had some thinking to do, mostly about his funeral-related promise.

He was sitting down on the bench with his new Bible and letting Elijah run around in the hope that he would get tired. He took the Bible out of the bag and realised that this was the first time he'd properly looked at one since the fire incident. This obviously wasn't the one he used to own. His previous one had been made using paper and had been surrounded by fire. There was little to no chance that he would be able to read it so he felt it best to get hold of another one.

Earlier that day he had managed to find a bookshop that was open and he purchased a Bible. He felt a bit strange doing it. He was standing in the section that all of the other religious books were shelved. They were all there together. They had all stood the test of time and they all had differing worths to different people. Within this section there were also the 'spiritual' shelves which included current day celebrities attempting to help people out with all of the intangible problems people might have. This included horoscopes, talking to the dead, quitting smoking through the language of the moon and how to pick a lucky name for your cat. Just the fact that they were all shelved next to each other made Stephen feel a warm shame rush through him and he hurriedly went to the till to get his book in a bag and get out of the general area.

He took it out and grazed his palm over the cover over the gold print of its title. Then he took out his pad of paper and a pen. He opened the Bible up and looked for some suitable passages.

He began highlighting and dog-earing some pages. As he was doing this he wondered several times how he got into this situation. It didn't make that much sense. He had never met the woman that he was meant to be finding a reading for but Sulky Barry was a sort of friend. And Sulky Barry didn't have that many friends. Come to think of it, maybe he was Sulky Barry's only friend. This thought made him sad, which was quite useful because he was writing for a funeral. He used it as fuel. He also decided to get into the mind-set of his old self before the smoke lifted his faith near his fiery house. He began writing of heavenly plains and God's general loveliness and how one looks down at one's own funeral and smiles at all those present celebrating a life. He would keep checking the piece of paper that he'd written down Barry's mother's name on to make sure he got it right for the speech. He eventually remembered without the aid of looking at the paper that her name was Sheila.

After struggling for a while with trying to personalise it, he concluded that that was Sulky Barry's job as he'd be the one doing the speech. He would just find a passage that vaguely covered the theme of getting to heaven and that would be close enough. Sheila was hardly going to be offended.

As he continued searching he noticed a shadow hover over his open Bible and then stop. It forced him to look up. The shadow belonged to a woman who was standing in the way of the sun which caused a strange glow to surround her head. It also meant that Stephen couldn't directly look at her and had to squint and avert his eyes. But he soon figured out that it was Flo that was standing before him and, through no fault of his own, he became exceedingly polite and happy.

'Oh, hi! It's you! I was wondering who that was, but it was you! How are you?'

'I'm fine, thanks,' she replied. 'Do you come here often?' They shared a chuckle at this cliché and she sat down next to him and inquired about what he was doing.

'Oh, I've been asked to find a reading for one of my work-friends. It's his mother's funeral. She was a Christian and so he asked if I could help. Hence...' and as he said this he closed the book and tapped twice over the words 'The Bible'.

'Ah. I see. I thought that it was bit odd you were reading that. That's sad news. When's the funeral?'

And soon they were talking naturally, sharing things with one another and doing polite things such as asking questions. It was Flo who decided to leave first.

'Well, it was good to bump into you but I've got to go and meet someone. I'll see you at the next meeting, though?'

'Yes. Definitely. Nice to see you too, Flo. See you soon.' And he watched her as she walked around the grass in the centre of the park and disappeared out of the entrance opposite him. He remained distracted as he attempted to continue preparing the speech. He felt as if she were still sitting next to him, watching him write. He still felt the place where she had touched him on the arm and he refused to move in case he lost it. Eventually he decided that he had something that could vaguely resemble a reading surrounded by some kind words and that he was simply wasting his time on the bench in the hope that she might walk back through the park again. So he returned to Wendy's.

Chapter 13

Their False Smiles Wore Thin In The Sleet

The funerals that take place within the teachings of Mooranity are strange affairs. Everyone attending the funeral must lean over the dead person and place their ear above the dead person's mouth. This comes from the tradition that states that a person must have taken their final breath before they are truly ready to depart from the land of mortals and can embark upon their quest for The Platinum Staircase.

Once everyone is in agreement that the body is ready to depart, it is placed on The Bench at the front of the temple for two days to make their journey that little bit easier. After this, their body is buried in the nearest forest so that if their journey was unsuccessful from The Bench, they'll still have a pretty good chance of finding The Staircase seeing as they're in a forest.

If this seems a little confusing and unclear then that is because it is clearly both of those things. However, it would be difficult to argue that when talking to a follower of Mooranity.

Then again, it is quite difficult to talk about most things with a follower of Mooranity without either offending them or entering a state of bewildered boredom that brings on fears that you might never get to leave the conversation.

Stephen, however, was attending a funeral that was based more around the Christian tradition. And it was, of course, much more sensible. Once everyone had spoken to the man that is omnipresent and asked him to let the nice old lady into his home, they would burn her body to ashes, pop them in a vase and then eat some cake.

'Lovely day for it!' said Stephen as he came down the stairs to the kitchen. Wendy was still in her dressing-gown, half-rushing for work.

'What was that, Stephen?'

'I said, "Lovely day for it".'

'What, for a funeral?' Then Stephen remembered that he had to go to a funeral today. Don't worry, he'd prepared and everything. It's not one of those situations. But he felt it best to explain this cheery mood that he'd related to the weather to Wendy. So he made something up.

'Well, yeah, wouldn't you rather be buried in nice weather? You wouldn't want all your friends and family getting wet as they say their last goodbyes, would you?'

'I suppose you're right.' He got away with it. 'Then again, maybe I would. Rain makes it all seem a bit more dramatic, doesn't it? I think I'd like a little bit of thunder and lightning as well,' said Wendy.

'That'd be pretty good, actually,' agreed Stephen. 'Alright. Well, I best be getting off. Could I nick that piece of toast?'

Immediately after he had finished driving to the funeral he had arrived at the funeral so he got out of his car and walked towards the crowd of people dressed in black. Stephen was greeted by Sulky Barry. His voice was much more quiet and sombre than normal as everyone's tends to be at a funeral. I am not necessarily saying this is a bad thing, this is just information for those that haven't been to a funeral and plan to show up and perform some of their most recently learned balloon animal tricks. Also, it's generally accepted that there won't be a magician that arrives on horseback. While this might be a lovely send-off that some people would love, many others aren't so keen on the idea of happiness at their funeral. Anyway, let's get on with what happened at the funeral Stephen had just arrived at. As I was saying, Barry's voice was much more quiet and sombre than normal.

'Hi, Stephen. Thank you so much for coming.'

'That's alright, Barry. Not a problem. Honoured I could be here.'

'I think we're starting any minute, so we may as well go in and you can get yourself all ready and the like.'

'Ready? Ready for what?' asked Stephen. This seemed to take Sulky Barry aback.

'For your speech, of course.'

'Oh, yeah, I brought the speech for you. It's here.' He began to remove some folded paper from his inside jacket pocket when Sulky Barry stopped him.

'Oh. No. I thought we established that you were doing a speech?' There doesn't tend to be much call for petty disagreements at funerals and, even though Stephen knew that he was, of course, correct, and that they had never made such an agreement, it seemed that he was now doing a speech in front of a group of strangers about a dead woman that he had never met. He had never been more terrified, including that one time when his house was on fire.

The crowd at the funeral weren't exactly a lively bunch. They filed in discretely to the church and found a seat. Stephen made sure he was on the end of a pew so that he could get up with ease to make his speech. He was in the perfect position when an amply proportioned late-comer arrived. She awkwardly squeezed in next to Stephen and half-apologised. Stephen began to explain that he was making a speech and needed to get out during the ceremony but he found this very difficult to do at the same time as remaining silent so he left the situation exactly as it was.

The vicar began speaking at the front.

'We are here today to commemorate the life of Sheila Mary Richards, a very kind and gentle soul. We wish her the very

best as she leaves this world and makes her way to the next.'
This kind of went on for a while.

The time eventually came when Stephen had to make his
speech. As he was standing up, he thought about how ridiculous
this was. He did know Barry. He was one of those friends that
was sort of a friend but that one wouldn't necessarily invite
around if you were inviting round 'the mates'. But then he
thought, 'Well, I'm here now. This is what is happening and
anyone who questions it is being a bit cynical about everyday
events. I mean, stranger things have happened…' The reason
this ellipsis occurred in Stephen's thought-process was because
he had arrived at the front of the church. This was after
having to force his way past the large lady that had sat next
to him. He had attempted this task in front of a group of
people struggling to act sombre while Stephen pretty much
sat on this woman's lap and slid across her to get out. When
he eventually managed to squeeze out of the pew without so
much as a titter from the funeral crowd, suggesting that all
human nature is repressed in such situations, he made his
way to the front in a falsely casual manner. He settled himself
before the funeral crowd and began to speak.

'Good afternoon. A lot of you won't know me but I'm Barry's
friend, Stephen.' As far as all these people were now concerned,
Barry and Stephen were friends. 'I've been asked to take a
reading from the Bible that I thought could offer us all some
solace at this time.' And he slowly opened his Bible after resting

it on the lectern. 'I have chosen something from Genesis 28: 10-18: "Jacob left Beersheba and set out for Haran. When he reached a certain place, he stopped for the night because the sun had set. Taking one of the stones there, he put it under his head and lay down to sleep. He had a dream in which he saw a stairway resting on the earth, with its top reaching to heaven, and the angels of God were ascending and descending on it. There above it stood the Lord, and he said: 'I am the Lord, the God of your father Abraham and the God of Isaac. I will give you and your descendants the land on which you are lying... I am with you and will watch over you wherever you go, and I will bring you back to this land. I will not leave you until I have done what I have promised you.'" He looked up from his reading to make sure that the message had landed successfully. He perused the crowd gathered to see a few soft nods, some tearful, some thoughtful, but all generally with an air of morose optimism after his reading. He closed the speech with some kind words and he picked up his Bible and sat back down. The woman didn't move up for him but, rather territorially, made him go past her again.

After the actual funeral bit with the speeches and stuff they all moved on to the local community centre to talk about things. It was there that everyone started thanking Stephen for his wonderful choice of a reading and his speech.

But, just as Stephen was getting used to the various groups of people surrounding him, he became very surprised when he found Brian standing there with a plastic plate covered in nibbles, gesturing a 'hello'.

'Brian! What are you doing here?'

'Well. I just wanted to see you in action, y'know?'

'Oh?' said Stephen. What had started out as simple surprise turned swiftly into deeply disturbed. So, naturally, he had to find out more. 'How did you know I was doing this?'

'Oh, you know. I've got my sources,' said Brian and he tapped his nose twice after placing a small sausage in his mouth as if this creepy boundary-cross of a social norm was just a bit of fun. Stephen felt compelled to break any silence that appeared so he asked more,

'So, you just came here to see how I gave my speech. You didn't know Barry's mother?'

'No, didn't know her. I just wanted to make sure you hadn't slipped back, that's all. I'm just keeping an eye on you. That was pretty moving stuff up there. You seemed very sincere. Did you mean it?'

'Well, of course I meant it, in a sentimental sense, that is. I didn't, you know, *mean* it mean it.' This seemed to cheer Brian up somewhat and he ate another small sausage jovially.

'Okay. No worries then. Although, I did really like your speech. I'm sure I'll take it on board and maybe try to apply it somewhere else.' Stephen didn't entirely understand what Brian meant by all of this but was more concerned by why the hell he was there anyway. Soon enough, after everyone had eaten a polite enough amount of cake so as not to be rude but not so much that they seemed to actually be comfortable and enjoying themselves, people gradually started to decide that it was time to go. Stephen took this opportunity to go as well. He was a sufficient amount of polite to Brian and Barry and he rushed out of the funeral.

After the funeral Stephen went back to Wendy's house. By the time he was back he was quite tired and did very little at all. He read the paper, watched TV, had some dinner, gave Elijah his and went to bed. I can't remember exactly how this happened but at some point, one way or another (most probably via the steady passing of time), Friday arrived.

Chapter 14

And Looked Down In Confusing Awe

I t was a Friday evening so it was time for another meeting. Stephen arrived once again with his bag and found the area outside the hall empty. He was worried he'd gone backwards after his steady progress over the past two weeks. But he was pleasantly surprised when he went inside to find seven people who had already set up a table and a set of chairs. As well as this, he found that they had a very large pad of paper on a plastic easel and an array of different coloured marker pens.

'Hello, Stephen. This is everyone. Everyone, this is Stephen,' said Brian gesturing around the group.

'Hello everyone,' said Stephen.

'Here we've got Flo and Matthew who you already know. Then we've got, help me out here,' he said to the group, 'Angela, is that right? Yes, Angela. Bobby, Mick, Jess, and is it David? Yes? And David.'

'Okay, brilliant. Thanks to everyone for coming. I'll try and remember all of those names.' Stephen felt a portion of pride wash through him as he looked around at this, admittedly, small crowd of people. 'I've created this,' he thought. And he saw that it was good.

'I've brought in this pad and some pens for us to use,' said Flo. 'I just thought it might be easier.'

'That's great,' said Stephen, 'thanks for that, Flo. That's going to be really useful.' They exchanged a small glance, one that is enough to suggest to you that they might be infatuated by each other a little bit but not enough of a look for you to be certain.

'Well then, we should probably get started. Last week we tried to settle some of the concerns that some people were having about the predicament of morals and the like so we decided it was best to put up some ideas.'

'Oh. You're not going to write them down again, are you, Stevey-boy?' interrupted Brian.

'Well I might not end up with the same list but I thought it'd be good to see what the new members...' exactly in the middle of this sentence Brian interrupted him.

'It's just that, I did the photocopying. I've got plenty here.'

'Oh. Well, there we are. Okay, I suppose that's easier.' Brian began handing out some sheets of paper. It turns out he had word-processed the list in the end and he was handing out all the copies that he had printed.

'Well,' said Stephen, clearly showing he wasn't totally sure about all of this but not enough to actually disagree. He had wanted it to be an open session so Brian's interest could only be a good thing. It was just that he wanted the new members to do some of their own thinking from the start. They weren't here to be told things again. But, instead of saying anything, he didn't.

'Murder,' said Brian jovially, 'not a very good idea.'

'Yep. I think they're aware of that, Brian,' said Stephen.

'Can't be too careful,' joked Brian. Brian continued his way through the list. The meeting was going just a little less than okay. At one point Mick put his hand up as if disagreeing but ended up asking when they would be starting the yoga. Stephen explained that they wouldn't. Mick asked whether this was the yoga lesson. Stephen explained that it wasn't. Mick left.

'Great,' said Stephen, a little overly enthusiastically, hoping they would be able to recover the meeting and continue unmarred by Brian's list reading.

'I'm quite happy to put that into some kind of a pamphlet if you like, Stevey-boy,' said Brian. 'Stevey-boy' was somewhat shocked by this unexpected suggestion so he felt it best to nip it in the bud as soon as possible.

'No, that's okay, Brian. That won't be necessary; they're more general guidelines, aren't they? People can make up their own minds, can't they?'

'Whatever you say, boss,' said Brian.

'Maybe we could go around the group like last time and find out a little about everyone and why they're here.'

Stephen worked his way around the group. Angela was Flo's friend who was just trying something out. Bobby had always felt this way but never felt like he had anyone to talk to. Mick had gone home to do some yoga.

Then Stephen got to Jess. He asked her some questions and found out a little about her. She was obviously not entirely comfortable being there. But then she shocked him with a very difficult question. A question that is quite difficult at the best of times:

'But... why?'

'Um... That's a bit vague if you don't mind me saying. What do you mean by 'why'?' he said.

'Well, before, right, when I used to, like, go to church, like, on a Sunday, right?'

'Oh no! Oh no no no no no!' thought Stephen, 'She's a 'right-like talker'. We've got a 'right-like talker', she'll never finish her point and then I'll have to decipher it.' His panic was cleverly kept internal. He was still unsure, however, whether her 'right?' was rhetorical or not and whether he should agree with her or prompt her. He decided the latter was the best option, just in case. So:

'Go on,' he said calmly.

'Well, it was always, like, sort of, you'll, like, go to heaven and stuff if you're, like, good and stuff. That's, like, your, like, reward for goodness.'

'She not that bad,' he thought, 'I can figure that one out,' and so he replied, 'So, what you're saying is: What's the point in being good if it's not getting you into heaven? Is that right?'

'Like, sort of, yeah.'

'Okay,' he said, and he took a moment. 'Well, in my opinion, it's because we can.' Some people looked a bit confused so he felt it best to explain what he meant. 'If you think about it, we obviously feel this need to be kind to one another because religions and moral standards tend to be based on that at their essence. It is something that we feel is generally and globally quite a good idea. The problem is that religion is so open to interpretation and, more than this, people feel so passionately about their religion that they see it as unadulterated truth. But without that element then we can just be nice. We don't have the unnecessary pride but we have all the good bits, the nice bits. You see what I'm saying? It's the same as pride in a nation but if we were to just step back and say, "Yeah, it's pretty nice living here but I wouldn't say it's the best place in the world. It's just alright and there's plenty of nice places with nice people that I don't really feel like offending or killing today," then wouldn't everything be just rosy and lovely? Anyway, it isn't as if this is *my* session, this is a collective after all, so that's a good question that's been raised by Jess, let's open it up for everyone.'

'They've got a binding place down the road. It's pretty cheap, I think. I walk past it every day on my way to work,' said Brian.

'What?' asked Stephen, obviously not on the same wavelength.

'A binding place. I could make those rules into a sort of folder.'

'Well, they're not rules, Brian, and I don't think we really need to worry about that. I thought we could open up this discussion a bit more.'

'You're right,' he lightly laughed. 'I'm sorry, I forget myself sometimes.'

'I wish I could forget you,' thought Stephen but then he brought himself back out of his mind and said, 'That's alright, Brian. Do you have an opinion on this issue?'

'I'm sorry. To be honest, I wasn't listening. I was trying to think what those little ropy things with metal bits on that go through a punched hole to turn it into a folder are called. What are those things called?'

'I'm not sure.'

'Oh, yeah, I know what you're talking about,' said Bobby, 'Yeah, what are they called?' They both sat there wondering while Stephen watched them in angered amazement.

'Not bulldog clips?' asked Bobby.

'No no,' said Brian, 'those are those really thick clips that come in different colours.'

'Oh that's right,' said Bobby, 'Yeah, wrong things.'

'Um,' said Flo suddenly, 'Sorry guys, but do you reckon we should get back to this?'

'Sorry. Sorry, I was off again, wasn't I?' said Brian in false self-effacement.

'Yes. Yes you were,' said Flo, reasonably calmly. And she continued the discussion as if without pointless interruption, 'I agree with Stephen on this one. We obviously have these good intentions in us. If we're able to do that with our own minds and with our own decisions then, surely, we can construct what is good and what is bad. If people across the world generally agree that murder is wrong then surely that tells you something.'

She was amazing. Or at least that's what Stephen thought. She was so strong and full of spirit. Her dark hair fell just below her shoulders but it also framed her face at the front. Her words sang through the depressing community centre and Stephen hung on to every one. He soon realised he was staring and stopped himself. The problem was that it was difficult to turn away without looking disinterested so he resolved to look back every now and again and not to stare. She saw that Brian was about to speak again so she asked him very quickly, 'Is it about stationery, Brian? Or is it about this issue? Because if it's about this issue then do go on.'

Brian paused briefly, tried to think his way out of it but had no such luck. He settled for,

'No, no, never mind.'

They all talked for a little longer. There were often points where Stephen would sit back for ten minutes at a time and just listen to people articulating all of the things that had worried him. All of his recent thoughts began to become organised in his head. He felt a purpose and he finally felt a little more happiness which had been in short supply of late.

After the meeting ended, they gathered outside in a small group before saying goodbye to one another as they all made their separate ways home. Brian located a match and struck it across the surface of the box it came in. He raised it to his lips where a cigarette was waiting to greet it. He partially shook the match and threw it to one side, letting it fall into a nearby drain. He noticed Stephen was walking away when he produced a small jog to catch up with him.

'Good meeting today, Stevey-boy,' said Brian as he caught up with Stephen and began walking alongside him.

'Yeah, it was alright,' he returned.

'It really is a good thing you're doing here, Stevey-boy. You're really helping people, y'know? I know for certain that you're helping me.'

'Well that's very kind of you to say. I don't like to think of it as me helping people. I think we're all helping each other.'

'Yeah, I suppose you're right. But just being part of it is good enough. I enjoy helping those people, y'know? There's something so fulfilling about it. I'd love to get more involved with the organisational side of it.'

Stephen looked across at the man in glasses who was walking next to him. Suddenly his head turned towards Stephen and he peered through the lenses with pleading eyes.

'Well, I don't really organise anything, as you know, we just all sort of turn up. But anything that you think would be useful or helpful would obviously be welcome.'

This cheered Brian up no end. His head turned back to the direction he was walking and a smile spread across his face.

'Thanks, Stephen. That means a lot. You know, after all your talk in the first meeting about how I can write about anything and that that can define who I am, I've just been totally inspired. I've really got back into the swing of putting time aside and just concentrating on my writing. You helped me do that Stephen and because of that you know I won't let you down.' He turned off in the direction of his house, as if his last sentence was an acceptable form of goodbye.

Stephen simply stood for a moment, watching the man as he breathed out more smoke which drifted over his shoulder which blended with the air around him before it disappeared. He felt an urge to simply watch this man turn another corner because he both frightened and fascinated Stephen. But mostly frightened.

Soon he was on his own and making the last part of his journey back to Wendy's house. An immense feeling of happiness began to rise inside him. He couldn't place what it was at first but eventually realised it was because he felt successful. He had organised something which was going well and it was his doing and he enjoyed it and he couldn't remember the last time that that sort of thing had happened to him. This feeling of happiness followed him home but then a new realisation hit him. Slowly, as he tried his best but couldn't get the face out of his mind, he realised that it might be partially to do with Flo as well.

Chapter 15

Answered With Bellowing Beauty

S hortly after Stephen's reasonably successful meeting, he arrived home.

Shortly after he went home, he got into bed.

Shortly after he got into bed, he went to sleep.

Shortly after he went to sleep, he woke up again.

Shortly after this, he had a weekend.

Shortly after this, he went to work. This involved going, being there, receiving another thank you from Barry, having a chat where Barry says that he notices that Stephen looks a little different and upset lately and offers him a pint at the pub followed by Stephen's usual refusal to do that sort of thing with anyone, except Wendy, of course. Stephen had to think of another excuse as to why he couldn't go and to wonder about why people keep doing that. This led him to conclude that the fault doesn't lie with other people and that perhaps he should take some time to really think about his own character and whether he should take some social jumps in the deep end, so to speak. He decided to put that on hold for a little bit, as he always did when it came to too much deep thought, and he decided it was time to go over to the park again, mostly because he liked it there. He also decided to take a book from Wendy's bookshelf, one that he'd been meaning to read for a little while after the fire incident. Shortly after making these decisions, he grabbed the book and went to the park.

Shortly after arriving in the park, he went for a little walk to his favourite bench and sat down. He looked briefly at the front cover of Charles Darwin's 'On the Origin of Species'.

He'd been sitting reading for a little while when someone that Stephen didn't like very much (and I'm sure you don't really like very much either) arrived in front of his little bench.

'Stevey-boy! Having a read in the park?' Stephen obviously knew exactly who it was without looking up but he looked up anyway and then he looked back at his book. And then he looked up again and he said,

'Yes. I *am* having a read in the park, Brian.'

Brian laughed jovially at this and said, 'Sorry. Bit redundant. What am I like!' He raised his cigarette to his mouth and then lowered it. His next words came out in the form of smoke as he said, 'What are you reading anyway?'

'On The Origin of Species.'

'Oh,' said Brian, seeming somewhat disappointed. 'Heavy stuff. I've never really cared for Darwin.'

'No? Have you read it? I don't think its main merits lie in its literary style, although that is good too. I think it's more the general theory that's important.'

Brian answered this very abruptly and very sure of himself, 'Oh, I know, I know that of course. I've just never cared for him generally.'

'Oh,' said Stephen. 'Well there we are then.' He felt it best to leave it there. He also felt it best to ask a question as equally inane as the one he had received on his arrival. 'So, are you just having a little stroll through the park?'

'Yes. Yes. I like to get a bit of exercise in, now and again, to get the old blood pumping, y'know?' he said as he raised his cigarette to his mouth again.

'Right you are,' said Stephen, feeling unsure if he'd ever used that phrase before and wondering whether he would use it again. He concluded that he actually quite liked it and he might use it again if the time came.

'We're not as young as we used to be, are we, Stevey-boy?'

'Right you are, Brian.' Coincidentally, the time had come now. But, more than anything, Stephen was trying to work out, in the nicest possible way, how long it would take for Brian to move on.

He felt the best way to play this was as a good chess player. Stephen was not a good chess player. Basically, he could play chess. Adding the word 'badly' to the end of the last sentence would be much fairer. However, he was aware that good chess players tend to think a few moves ahead and really good ones look many more than that ahead. Really, really good chess players can see the final move before the first one has even been taken but nobody likes playing them so we don't tend to see them exercise this skill. Stephen decided to play conversational chess with Brian. He thought this through very quickly. He had a thought process where he worked backwards from his final and desired result. It went something like this:

Brian leaves.

Why?

He says he better be off.

Why?

He has somewhere to go.

Where?

I better ask him.

He was just about to do what his brain had told him to when he suddenly felt a sneaky chess move coming on. It was a bit like when one is playing chess and is about to move a piece and everything looks fine but a realisation hits at the last second when one sees a knight lurking behind a rook. Are we taking this chess simile too far? 'Yes' is the answer you are definitely looking for. But I can only report what Stephen was thinking at the time. He definitely saw a conversational knight lurking. The knight was this:

'If I ask him where he's going he might say where and invite me. Or he might say nothing and see whether I fancy going to the pub. I should take a different approach.'

Now, I realise that this whole thought process is taking a very long time and there would have been a lot of silence during this time where Stephen was looking at Brian and making imaginary chess moves. But actually the situation outside Stephen's tactical mind was very different. Brian was explaining several reasons why he didn't like Darwin and his theory very much and Stephen was nodding with vigour. As well as this, Brian was explaining that he feels the thoughts that they've been laying down (or, as he had started insisting on calling them, 'guidelines') for the past couple of weeks need a bit of finalising, 'perhaps a bit more metaphor, maybe more motive. It just makes it a bit more interesting, doesn't it? I don't know. We'll kick around some more ideas next week,' were some of the things Brian was happily saying. Stephen wasn't really listening. But, luckily, Brian was quite content in continuing on his talking with no interruption. This left Stephen plenty of time to think up some more chess moves.

How do I make him say he's got something on?
I can't.
Shit.

Was this checkmate? No. It couldn't be. Was he stuck there? But then he had a wonderful revelation: How could he have been so foolish? Why did Brian have to leave? Why couldn't Stephen just leave? Why didn't he give up his bench and his reading time and his pleasant time in the park and pretend to be going somewhere?

At first he thought, 'No. I was enjoying myself, I was enjoying the calm of reading in the outdoor air, I was enjoying the sound of the birds and watching their ability to fly in awe, I was enjoying the rustle of the trees as their branches sway in the wind, I was enjoying the sound of the distant trickle of water which is weird because we're nowhere near a river. Why should I give up that enjoyment just to avoid an awkward conversation?' But then he left his mind briefly just to hear a bit of what was going on. Brian was still explaining some of his ideas about the next meeting and this made Stephen come to a more rigid conclusion. He thought, 'Sod it. Nothing's worth this.'

'Actually, sorry Brian. I better be off actually. I said I'd meet one of my old schoolmates. Haven't seen him in years. Just looking at the time,' he pretended to look at his watch, 'Yeah, thought so, I'm late as it is.'

'Oh, that's not a problem, Stevey. We can walk and talk.'

Checkmate.

Not long after Stephen had given up with a, 'Yeah, we could,' he found himself walking towards a fake dinner meeting with his old school friend who he had decided to call John. In his panic he hadn't even thought of someone who was actually a schoolmate but instead made someone up.

The problem with lies is that they grow. It's fine if they're small but the more layers that are added, the harder it is for the liar to keep up with what he or she has lied about. So Stephen decided to keep it simple. John was now the new name for his schoolmate Robbie and, if anything more came up about him, he'd be able to just talk about him. Unfortunately it did come up.

'So was John a close mate of yours?' asked Brian.

'Yeah, pretty close. He was in my sort of 'group' or 'gang' or whatever you want to call it.'

'Gang, eh?' said Brian, as if Stephen had said it with conviction which, if you refer to the last sentence, you will know that he didn't. 'Carried around baseball bats and knuckle-dusters, did you?' His belly laughed and his mouth followed suit. Stephen feigned a titter and said, 'Something like that.' They continued to walk side by side along the pavement. If you would like to understand this further then perhaps you would like to re-enact this scene with someone. It is best to ask them first. I do not encourage you to simply start walking beside someone as if you know them. This is very strange and odd behaviour that I would have to discourage simply because I would feel very uncomfortable and confused if anyone did this to me.

As they were walking they continued talking at the same time. 'What does your mate do now, then?'

'Something in insurance, I think. I really haven't spoken to him in ages. That's why I'm looking forward to catching up.' He'd added another layer and even just one layer threw him off balance, 'He phoned me up, out of the blue, and I was like, "Robbie? Is that you?" It was really weird.'

'I thought you said his name was John.' There was a deathly silence. Stephen swallowed and struggled to find a clever explanation. He failed.

'Yeah, uh, Robbie was his nickname.'

'Why was that?' inquired Brian.

'Well... It's because he looked a bit like Robbie Williams.' 'Fantastic!' he thought, 'Why didn't I think of that?' and then he remembered that he did. And that was part of the problem as Brian said,

'What? When you were in school? You're a bit older than when his career got into full swing, aren't you?'

There was that silence again. Stephen noticed he was near a restaurant.

'Well here we are!' he said, his voice just about managing not to give away the horrible panic he was feeling. Brian looked at him and appeared to forget the obvious lie and the fact that Stephen had totally ignored his last enquiry as he said.

'Oh, alright. Well, have fun catching up with John or should I say Robbie?'

'Yeah,' Stephen laughed slightly, 'I'm sure I will. I'll see you next week, Brian.' And he wandered inside.

'Have you got a reservation, sir?' came the very efficient Italian accent as he entered.

'Um, well, no.'

'Well, I am afraid we are all full up at the moment, and we have no tables free for 45 minutes at least.'

'No, no, that's fine. I don't want to eat here.'

'Then why are you in here?'

Shame washed through Stephen's body. A shame based on bad lying, a shame based on poor conversational chess anticipation, a shame based on partaking in conversational chess in the first place and then just an extra helping of shame from somewhere else that he couldn't really place.

'I don't know,' he said.

Chapter 16

This Incredible Beast

'Yeah, I suppose. As long as they realise they're not actually going there, I'm willing to accept it,' said Stephen.

That was weird, wasn't it? I thought I'd try out a new technique of starting the chapter more abruptly. I'm going to spend the next little while working towards that first sentence up there. Normally this technique is done over an entire story rather than in a chapter. It is particularly unusual for it to happen in Chapter 16. It's near enough unheard of in fact. You'll know when I've arrived at that sentence because I'll write it again. I bet you can't wait to find out what it's all about now. I wouldn't bet any money on it; perhaps my pride or something equally useless.

Another meeting had arrived. Stephen was standing in front of the over-sized pad of paper on the easel. This time he'd picked a dark blue pen to write with. There were a lot more people that evening. Well over sixteen, I would say. They had been introduced and nearly all of them had names and there was an open discussion occurring to do with motivation for morality again.

'Well we're here aren't we? We've obviously survived,' said a man with a name. 'If we've survived then teamwork has obviously worked for us so far. We should carry on, it just makes sense.' Stephen wrote 'SURVIVAL' down on the over-sized pad.

'Yeah, I agree. Survival's a big one. Any more?'

'Just being nice?' There was a small, endearing chuckle from the group. It was quite a lovely atmosphere. You would have loved it there, I assure you. Stephen finished his section of the collective small, endearing chuckle and he wrote 'BEING NICE' down and said,

'I entirely agree again.'

'It's just that,' came an interrupting voice that belonged to a person that you would probably guess the name of, 'there's still no *real* motivation.'

'What's that, Brian?'

'We're coming up with possible reasons we're moral and possible reasons why we should be but there's no actual, proper motivation.'

'Do we need one?' said Flo. 'Surely it's quite selfish to need one.' Stephen had momentarily forgotten that Flo was there but she sprung back into his view and suddenly she was all he could think of. His infatuation was making his power in the meetings even more depleted. There was a small murmur of agreement through the group. Stephen couldn't tell whether this was agreeing with Flo's rhetorical stance or agreeing with

Brian that, yes, we do need one. Unfortunately, it seemed some were leaning towards the more frightening latter.

'Sorry, Flo, is it?' Brian said, 'I think Katie was about to speak.' He looked across at Katie and it became most apparent that she wasn't even remotely about to speak but he used the opportunity he created to continue his thought process as if uninterrupted, 'It's just, you know, maybe we don't call it heaven. Maybe we call it... Oh, I don't know...'

'The Island?' came a voice from a person with a name.

'I like it, yeah. So, when discussing it, it's more conceptual, y'know? Kind of metaphorical but it just gives some more structure, some more imagination, y'know? Just kind of a better...' he searched for the word in his mind. The way he looked back at Stephen, one would have thought that he'd thought of a brilliant word. He hadn't. He concluded his sentence with the vague and annoying 'vibe'. Stephen was stunned. He didn't really know what to do. But he felt a wave of quiet agreement coming from the group and he didn't really feel like arguing with this many people about a conceptual idea.

'Um... Well. Do you think?' He showed his hesitation but obviously not enough.

'Where's the harm?' said Brian, fixing him with his eyes.

'Yeah, I suppose. As long as they realise they're not actually going there, I'm willing to accept it,' said Stephen.

There we go, we arrived at the sentence eventually. I hope it added a further layer to it.

'So,' he continued, 'how and why, would you say, hypothetically, you might make your way to this island?'

'Um… Stephen?' said Brian.

'Yes?'

'I think we agreed on *The* Island.' Stephen paused. Checkmate again.

'Um, yeah, okay,' he said and he slowly and hesitantly wrote it on the paper.

Perhaps you would have dealt with this differently. Perhaps it is clear that Brian was being a complete arse and he should have been stopped before he takes this somewhere it shouldn't go. Perhaps that is totally correct. Actually, it's definitely correct and I know Stephen would agree if he still could. It's just that it wasn't really in his nature to bring something like that up. He continued to let it slide. He continued to let Brian bully him into strange agreements.

He was more taken aback by how strange they were becoming but he did nothing to stop it and I know for a fact he would regret it and change it if he could. Unfortunately, I am to tell you what really happened rather than what Stephen would have liked to have happened. I suppose what he would have liked to have happened was simply to create a little solace for people like him. To carry on his life as a normal person who just bumbled along and had small bits of enjoyment interspersed with the slightly less enjoyable moments that create a balance, making the happy moments seem happier.

That was really all he wanted. Unfortunately, that might be the exact opposite of what he got.

That last sentence was there to create suspense. Just thought you'd like to know.

Chapter 17

The Mighty Hand That Guides You There

S tephen and Wendy felt it best to head over to the park with Elijah. This was shortly after Stephen had come home from the meeting and begun to try and explain his worries, vexations, problems and fears to Wendy. Because he was trying to explain all of these at once he got a bit confused. He was finishing sentences half-way through and then starting half-way through another. Trying desperately to keep up with his haphazard thought-process, Wendy felt it best to calm him down and take a walk in the park while slowly letting it all leak out of him.

'Yeah. That sounds like a good idea, Wendy.'

'Ok. I'll just grab my coat.' She put on her long jacket that Stephen liked to call her fashionable spy jacket. As they left the house Stephen said something along the lines of,

'Don't you find we're going to the park a lot? Normally for very little reason at all.'

'I know, it's not very imaginative, is it?' said Wendy or something along those lines as she gently closed the door behind her.

It seems we've just been locked inside the house. But don't worry, let's just walk up to the boring-coloured door, lower the latch and leave the house as well. If we just close the door quietly then Wendy need never know we were there and we could still catch up with them down the road.

After walking a little along the pavement, Stephen avoiding the cracks, Wendy quite willing to stand on them and Elijah seeming to take the longest possible route along the straight pavement, they found they were walking in the park. They meandered their way along the path in silence for a while but it was the kind of silence where the people were perfectly okay about it. It was just silent.

It was Wendy who broke the silence.

'So, tell me about this meeting. What's troubling you?' Her eyes looked a reasonable level of wise, they pierced Stephen's. She was taking on the air of a psychiatrist and she was really enjoying herself.

'Well, it's, sort of, all gone wrong.' He had started off as positively as he could. And Wendy settled into her 'I'm listening' role. 'I mean there's this guy, you know Brian, don't you? And he's kind of taken over but I'm not worried about power or anything, it's nothing like that, it was my idea, though. But I do want a collective and he's part of that collective and it's not up to me to change people, is it? People are who they are and all that kind of thing, y'know? And it's all changed. We're writing stuff down and they used to be just ideas, small things to discuss. It was just a place to meet people in the same boat but now these things are almost becoming rules. They're very nice rules but surely we shouldn't be laying down rules. Then again, that is what the group wanted and who am I to stand in their way. I'm just all over the place. I'm really confused. What should I do? Is it even up to me to do anything? I just… I'm so…'

'Whoa! Whoa, there! Now, this is why we came here. You were going to calm down and speak slower and try to finish each train of thought before attempting another, remember? Let's do this one at a time,' said Wendy.

'You're right,' said Stephen, slightly embarrassed, 'Sorry. It just all came pouring out, didn't it? Okay. Let's start with Brian, shall we?'

'I can't wait,' she lied. Stephen realised this.

'No, wait. I shouldn't be bothering you with all this. You don't have to, honestly.'

'No, no. I was joking. Honestly, I want to hear. We're friends, aren't we? "A problem shared" and all that. Come on, let's hear it.' Stephen hesitated for a moment and then he pressed on.

'Okay, Brian.' He went on to explain a lot of things that we're already aware of. There's not really much point in me boring you with any of it after you've already heard it all once and you might not have even enjoyed hearing about it the first time around. If that is the case then I apologise greatly. That's not the main point anyway, this is all just very important. But, if you're willing to continue, Wendy was in a 'happy and understanding' type of mood and an 'I'll partially sort out all of this' mode. We join her laughing.

'So, you actually went into the restaurant?'

'Yeah, it's pretty bad.'

'I'd say so. It's pretty funny, though.'

And then they got back to laughing. Not too much because it wasn't that funny.

'Anyway,' continued Wendy as they sat down on their bench, 'You're right. This was a good idea of yours that you've watched blossom over the past few weeks but perhaps it is time to just see how things take their course. I know you're not the kind to try and seize control. You're not an angry person. Why be something you're not? Especially when the thing you aren't is an irritating person. Obviously, if the thing you weren't was a nice person then I'd encourage you to rethink some things. But that's advice for someone else. Anyway, where was I? Oh yeah, perhaps this Brian guy is a bit of an idiot.'

'Can I stop you there?' interrupted Stephen, 'He definitely is.' They both laughed and Wendy continued.

'Okay. So this Brian guy is a bit of an idiot. But if that's true, then someone or all of you will make that known and obvious soon enough. Things like this have a way of working themselves out.'

'That's your solution for nearly everything.'

'I know. It's based on a mixture of a love of laziness and a desire to do nothing. But it's probably founded in idealism somewhere in the background.'

'I'm sure it is.'

'How cynical of you, Stephen,' said Wendy, 'You don't see me as an idealist?'

'Oh, don't get me wrong, you are an idealist. But like you said, a lazy one.'

'That's very true!' she said, 'What about you? I think you're a much bigger idealist than me.'

'Maybe just one who doesn't deal with obstacles very well.'

'I think most idealists are lazy,' said Wendy. 'But then people who aren't idealists are also lazy. The problem is that those that aren't get to win because if you're not an idealist then you can just leave everything as it is. So, even if you're lazy, you still win. So, in conclusion,' she stood up in mock dramatics, 'we are the lazy species!' and she pointed upwards as if making a very important speech. Almost as important as this book. 'We sit whenever we can. We will always strive for easier and easier ways to get food into our stomachs. If drips were more readily available we would take them, no questions asked. Yesterday, I watched three property shows in a row because the remote was too far away. And that is what laziness is. It is about perception, everything is too far away. Much too far away. The world is getting smaller but it is still not small enough. It will never be small enough for the lazy species!' Stephen laughed at her and gave a clap and made crowd 'whooping' noises as she bowed and then sat down.

'You're quite right. Us and the sloth,' said Stephen. Wendy chuckled along with him.

'That's right. Us and the sloth. But at least their laziness is built in. We've just become lazy. If you want some evidence,

I give you… the Drive-Thru. We're too lazy to get out of the car and go inside to eat somewhere. The epitome of human laziness.'

'Right you are,' he said again.

'Right you are? Where's that come from.'

'Oh, sorry, it's just something I've started saying.'

'Since when?'

They talked for a little longer but I don't want to pry too much into their conversation. Even though I am telling you Stephen's story, it would be quite rude to watch him all of the time. Maybe a little bit of privacy is called for here.

Let's just take a moment.

Okay, I'm sure that's long enough. Let's see what they're talking about.

Oh. They've gone home. But there is a man sitting on the bench. He looks nice enough and he doesn't look likely to abandon us. Perhaps at some stage I could tell his story as well. But it's not nearly as important as Stephen's. So, if you don't mind, I'm going to carry on with his. What's more, we've invested so much time in Stephen's that it would be a shame not to find out what happened. Oh look. There goes Flo wandering past the man on the bench. You do get the feeling that she's lovely, don't you? I really hope she gives Stephen a chance because he's definitely lovely. We'd better just go and find him. He'll probably be at home by now. I apologise. I let my guard down for a second. This is very poor storytelling. Don't worry, my thinking is I'll just let the chapter end here and hopefully I'll have found him by the beginning of the next one.

Chapter 18

The Lower Reaches Cried

Stephen took Wendy's advice on board but there was still something bothering him. He had created this. What had all of this become?

It's all getting quite serious now, isn't it? Unfortunately, this does tend to be the mood from here on. What started out as harmless fun (apart from Malcolm the fire but even he had a friendly name) seems to be getting more sinister, I'm sure you'll agree. The thing is, and I feel I really must make this clear, this is all very important and I can only convey what actually happened. I might try to break up all the seriousness with a foolish thought here or there. Even though I'm not known for doing that, I will see what I can do.

So Stephen went along to the next meeting and tried to hold two conflicting thoughts in his head at once. He struggled to do this so he made them into one thought based on 'if's and 'but's. By this I mean he was trying to hold these two conflicting thoughts in his mind at the same time:

1. This is all getting out of hand. What have I done? I should stop this.

2. Maybe it's still just harmless. These people can think what they want to think. It's up to them. I don't have to think along with them. I shouldn't stop this.

The way that he managed to rationally make these incompatible thoughts work together was:

I will go along and play things by ear. I will see what it's like. These people are responsible for their own thoughts and feelings and it's not up to me but if I see it all getting too out of hand I might say something.

He arrived to find even more people than a reasonably intelligent one and a half-year-old could count. He looked around and saw that one of the other reasons he was there was sitting on her own and he walked towards an empty seat next to her.

'Hi, Flo,' he said casually as he sat down next to her.

'Oh, hi!'

'So…' it was no good. He had nothing to follow. Not even the obvious one. But then it came screaming back to him. 'How are you?'

'I'm good. You?'

'I'm good as well! Coincidence!' This was all getting a bit much for Stephen. He'd never been good at this in any way and today was no exception. He resolved that he would ask her where she lived but then that seemed a bit creepy. He sat looking just to the left of her as if searching for the answer out of the window. He had nothing more to say.

'Maybe I should just ask her out somewhere,' he thought but then he quickly decided against such an insane idea.

Stephen's lack of speech was interrupted by the arrival of more people through the door. One of these, unfortunately, was Brian. But as Stephen looked at all the other people that were making their way in, the pride he had originally felt because of the slowly growing amount of people was fading.

They had cleverly pushed together four tables to make one big table. It is a universal law that, even when you push four tables together, what you have created is still just a table. This suggests that, to many people, no matter how many tables make up a table, a table is a table is a table. Most people prefer not to worry about these sorts of things and just grab a chair. These are the sort of people that can't handle stopping reading mid-word and coming back in a week's time.

'Ah, Stevey-boy!' came the familiar voice. Brian was standing up for everyone to see him. 'Sorry, no. Best not start off like that. Too familiar. Everyone, this is Stephen Moore. Stephen, this is everyone.' Just as this introduction was offered yet another person walked through the door. 'Hello! Welcome. Come and sit down. This person is also part of the "everyone" that I just mentioned. Everyone, including the person that just came in, this is Stephen. He sort of runs this joint, isn't that right, Stephen?' and he feigned a kind of shadow-boxing punch towards Stephen who was forced to feign a shadow-boxing guard and block of some kind. Brian tried to carry on with a massive smile on his face but Stephen felt it very necessary to say,

'Right, shall we crack on?'

What they did almost immediately after Stephen had uttered these words was 'crack on'. Brian flipped over the front cover of the over-sized pad and revealed what had been written last week. Stephen was very keen to prevent starting in this manner from becoming a habit. He'd only really written these to settle peoples' fears that they were lost without their old way of life. He told them all this.

'Um. Yeah. We wrote those out just to create a common ground. No, not that. It was just to show that we can be moral without being told morals. We can make up our own minds, you know?' A few people seemed to understand. They began nodding but then Brian interrupted.

'Yeah, that's it. I had a chat with a few people at the end of the last meeting and they liked them a lot. That's why I thought it would be a good idea to give out these.' He was in the middle of saying 'these' as his head disappeared under the table before emerging again followed by his arms lifting up a large box file. He opened it up while everyone waited to see what he would reveal. He pulled out a big pile of what looked like leaflets. On further analysis, they would be best described as something that was thicker than a leaflet but thinner than a book. I believe scientists call them pamphlets. They were passed around the group and this began to create small noises of excitement and gratitude. As if someone had just put on a mildly impressive fireworks display. 'These are really good, Brian. Did you make these yourself?' and such remarks were uttered around the group. Stephen was beyond shocked when he looked down at the pamphlet as it arrived in front of him on the table. It read:

JUST SOME THOUGHTS ON HOW WE SHOULD LIVE OUR LIVES.

The thought that he had arrived at the meeting with had been set off in his head; both his 'if' and 'but' had been alerted and he realised it best to try and say something.

'Um, Brian?'

'Yes, Stevey-boy?'

'Well, these pamphlet things. They're very good and everything.'

'Thank you very much.' Brian had obviously never heard anyone do the 'and everything' end to a sentence which suggests that the first part of the sentence was not the opinion they were trying to convey at all. He took it as the whole sentence and carried on unaware. 'Glad you like them,' he said. 'Don't worry; you get some credit in there.' Stephen became more shocked than during his state that I previously described as beyond shocked.

'Well, thanks,' lied Stephen. 'It's just, well; I don't really feel comfortable with this, to be perfectly honest, Brian.'

'What? Come on now, Stevey-boy. It's harmless enough. Don't worry yourself. I've only expanded them a bit. Made them a bit clearer, y'know?'

'I realise that,' he continued. 'It's just that this feels somewhat like... ruling people and I'm not sure if I'm totally comfortable with the general idea of ruling people.'

'Don't be silly, Stevey,' said Brian and then he turned to the group. 'You don't feel like we're ruling you, do you, guys?' Everyone shook their head and agreed at the same time.

Stephen could definitely have done more. Stephen definitely should have done more. But, unfortunately, Stephen definitely didn't do more. Instead he looked around at how happy people seemed to be and looked down at what he'd received from Brian and began reading it to find out what this was all about.

For the rest of the meeting there was little discussion about anything else apart from the pamphlet and its contents. There was no open discussion about morality, belief, science, logic or anything of the sort. Rather, they spent half an hour looking through and discussing what Brian had written. The first page was a contents page, the second an introduction to Stephen and some contact information and the third was a kind of general welcome and some information about the time and days of meetings. But then it got a bit worse. If I were to be dramatic, I would write another sentence after that one that read 'Much worse.' but I don't want to. After the reasonably pleasant and ominous title of 'Just some thoughts on how we should live our lives', pages four and five were less pleasant and more ominous. Stephen entered into a state that was more shocked than the state of shock that I said was beyond the state of shock earlier. The top of page four read 'The Laws We Live By.' Below it were expanded versions of what had been discussed in previous meetings.

But there was more. There were some written accounts of previous meetings. Some things that were discussed were written down as brief bullet points. One included a very questionable word, see if you can spot it:

'As discussed in some of the meetings, we are still open-minded about the idea of an "un-pin-down-able mystery" that accompanies our lives. As we were aware of that concept in our previous thoughts and it is present all over the world, we cannot rule it out, even though it is something we might question.'

Stephen could not tell exactly what this vague sentence was trying to say. Whether it was calling this vague 'mystery' the irrational thing it was or whether it was accepting it. But he was suddenly distracted by another thing that was written:

'The idea of having more substance to believe in is something that we are yet to establish. This will arrive through group discussion but we cannot rule out the idea of people or objects that can help us in gaining a better understanding of the inner workings of ourselves.'

What did this even mean? It was even vaguer than the last one. Stephen was about to protest but people were too busy discussing this very point. He was very nearly almost going to interrupt but the words 'very', 'nearly' and 'almost', when used together, generally mean no action at all takes place. Stephen simply remained sitting, dumbstruck and unable to do anything much whatsoever.

Stephen's shock that was beyond the state of shock that was beyond the state that was beyond shock persisted. This rendered him pretty useless for the rest of the meeting. So useless that he said very little else. He did not protest. He did not question. He just let it all unfold in front of him before going home to stare at a wall for a bit while his mind struggled to keep up with itself.

Chapter 19

Fortune and Fate

You'll never guess where Stephen went after all of this. He was alone and upset. Wendy was out with some friends so Stephen attached a lead to Elijah's collar and wandered, very obviously, over to the park. He felt suddenly very calm as he sat on his bench. He heard the birds, he heard the trees and he saw the pages of his book ripple as the wind rushed lightly through them. His heart rate settled and he got things into perspective.

There are certain points where one can feel as though one has let everything go. This isn't true; of course, because no one will ever be at the point where they don't have anything they have to do. It's just that sometimes one can trick oneself and can sit on a bench in a park and feel the stress flow out of them like a watery thing.

The point is that there is never a time when we don't have something to do and it seems relatively important to make the time to do other things that put a little smile on our face now and again. These can include: eating a sandwich, looking at a cat, discussing with someone what you would do if you won the lottery and imagining a cat. Stephen had the feeling that looking at a cat can bring as he sat in the park, watching the sun cling to the final moments of the day as it slowly slipped behind the horizon.

There was next to nothing that could force that moment to completely turn around and make Stephen tense up like a suddenly alert meerkat but that next to nothing event occurred as Stephen heard a certain voice and he felt the air around him begin to fill with tobacco smoke. He didn't mind the smell of tobacco smoke nor did he mind smoking generally but it became very apparent that recently he had begun to hate it and it was only because he associated it with the man that was about to speak.

'Reading him again, are we Stephen?'

Stephen wasn't one to swear overly. He found this was because he wasn't a very convincing swearer. There was something lacking in his commitment to the words. So, he worked on a policy of saving swear words up and then, when he used them, they have much more impact. Stephen felt the time was right and, 'what's the fucking point?' was what he thought.

'Hiya, Brian' was what he actually vocalised. 'How's it going?'

'Not too bad. Listen, I didn't mean to annoy you with those pamphlets or anything, Stephen. I didn't think you'd mind.'

'Oh. Don't worry about it. I'm just a bit tired,' he lied. In fact, this was the sixteenth most awake he had ever been.

His heart was beginning to pump faster and louder. He thought that Brian might be able to hear it, it was so loud. Adrenaline brought on by anger was speeding up his blood-flow considerably.

'Well, that's good to hear. Because I've got plenty of ideas for the next meeting. If that's alright with you, of course.' His heart was getting quicker.

'Yeah, of course, Brian. It's a collective discussion place after all.'

'That's great,' said Brian. 'So how was John the other day?'

Stephen had forgotten his layer of lies.

'John?'

'I'm sorry. *Robbie* if you'd prefer!'

'Oh, sorry, yeah. I never think of him as John. Yeah, Robbie was fine.' He was definitely doing this properly this time, he wasn't going to let there be a checkmate scenario again.

'Listen, sorry Brian, mate,' he began, 'Going to have to shoot off again. I'm heading back home for some dinner. But I'm sure I'll see you around the park soon enough!' He joked about this as if he was mildly pleased about the fact. He called Elijah over and re-attached his lead.

'Yes, I'm sure you will.' laughed Brian. 'Oh, I look forward to telling you about my ideas at the next meeting,' he was saying as the two began parting ways. Stephen continued to walk away, he wasn't going to stop.

'Oh, yeah, I look forward to hearing about your ideas,' said Stephen, having to get louder. As he walked backwards he almost tripped over a dodgy bit of the path.

While Stephen was learning why people should not talk and walk backwards and why having eyes facing in the direction we generally walk in is a good idea, he was almost entirely unaware that on Friday's meeting Brian would be revealing his ideas about The Platinum Staircase.

Chapter 20

Everyone Grimaced And Went Inside

Stephen's story really seems to be taking a turn for the worse. I know some people may be pin-pointing the reason for this as Brian. He's somewhat manipulative, I'm sure you'd agree. It could even be possible that you'd say Brian is to blame for everything that's gone wrong since the marble boys reared their naïve heads. Perhaps even before then. But blame is hardly overly helpful. I think there are some other things going on here. Some very important things.

But to step away from that for a second, I thought that there was a character that has been neglected for a little while, mostly because he doesn't get up to much. So let's revisit him and find out what he's doing. After his visit to the park with Stephen, Elijah was taking a wander around Wendy's back garden, sniffing various spots that he'd forgotten he'd already sniffed earlier, when he found that by jumping to a certain height he could lower the handle of Wendy's side gate and find his way out onto the pavement of the street. He decided to explore. Of course he didn't so much 'decide' in the way that we do, but the chemical signals in his brain set his curious feet off in an exploring manner.

He began sniffing his way along fences and down alleys, urinating on whatever he decided to lay claim on. Stephen took him on walks, as the more attentive readers may know, but Elijah decided to go on a different route to normal this time around. For a description of how he 'decided' see the previous paragraph.

He found himself in a dead-end road, surrounded by houses. People were inside, unaware of one another's lives. They were doing whatever they wanted to do and that was fine by everyone else. He wandered past a window and, even though he didn't understand the concept, he witnessed a man named Mick practising his yoga.

He walked past another window, this one had some siblings watching the television and arguing over who got to be the car in a board game. Before long, he came to a window where a man was looking out at a dog. The man was previously just looking out at the street with a cigarette in his hand. This hand was being used very efficiently as it was also propping up his head and forcing his thick glasses to create a wonky angle in front of his face. That was until Elijah showed up and it would be perfectly fair to say that, at the exact moment that he arrived, the man was looking at a dog.

The man was at his desk. He'd been scrawling various ideas onto bits of paper and sporadically looking up and out of the window to gather his thoughts. At the moment that Elijah found himself padding his way through the dusk breeze, a voice came through the slightly opened window that belonged to the man inside.

'Of course,' it said. 'The Platinum Staircase!' and he saw that it was good.

Elijah's travels eventually ended as he found his way back into Wendy's garden. No one knew that he had gone and he had already partially forgotten most of it himself. He walked into the kitchen and was greeted by the offer of some food in his bowl and a scratch on his belly. Life was good.

After Elijah's semi-adventure ended, Stephen was sitting in the living room with his arms crossed, deep in thought and letting the light from the television beam over him. Wendy came in with Elijah who promptly hopped onto the chair that he had gradually made his own. Wendy sat down next to Stephen and looked at him. He saw her looking at him out of the corner of his eye.

'What?' he said.

'Oh. Nothing. It's just that you're clearly thinking about something.'

'How would you know?'

'I don't know. Maybe it's the way you're sitting. Maybe it's the fact that you're not really watching the TV, you're just sitting in front of a programme that you've told me you hate and I bet you couldn't tell me anything about what's happened in the past five minutes because you're not even paying attention.'

'I could tell you. That girl there has told that guy that she never wants to see him again because he said something nasty about her mum.'

'Have you made that up?'

'No.'

'I'll find out during the omnibus. But in the mean time, tell me what's up.' Stephen took a little moment; he didn't want to admit that he was troubled or that Wendy was right about not paying attention to the television. But Wendy was definitely the one he could talk to nowadays.

'I don't think I want to go to the next meeting.'

'Then don't,' she said, helpfully.

'It's not as simple as that.'

'Bugger. I was really hoping I'd solved that one.' This made him chuckle a bit.

'It's still the same thing. That Brian guy, y'know? I think he's getting worse. There was something very ominous about what he said in the park earlier and I'm really curious about what he's going to do next time.' Stephen had become a bit more perceptive lately and he was definitely right to be a little worried this time around.

'Well, then. Go,' said Wendy.

'Thanks,' he said. 'I can always rely on you.'

'Don't mention it. Now, can we please change the channel because their conversation is only slightly more boring than ours and I think I need something a little less dull?'

'I like your thinking.' Stephen changed the channel and found a comedy panel show. They were both reasonably happy with this and giggled at the appropriate moments.

Time passed. Day became night which in turn became day. Events occurred around the world, some important, some not. People were being born and people were dying. Some were getting married, some divorced. Some were playing music, others listening to it. Some were reading books and were unsure about whether they liked them or not. I think you get the idea. This whole time, the life of the man that we're following also continued as it tended to. This included working at his unimportant job and worrying in his friend's house. He walked his dog through the park, he ate food, he neglected learning to play his trumpet and he generally got on with life. Or at least the part of his life that was the particular week I'm discussing.

Eventually the meeting that he'd deliberated over arrived. He was lost, though. Not in the sense that he was physically lost, it wasn't that far and he'd made his way there many times before. He was mentally lost. He was going to another meeting with little understanding of how he was going to play things this week. He concluded, for the sake of his sanity more than anything else, that he would take much more of a back-seat than normal. He'd always called it a collective and he would still try to initiate things to get things going but this week he was leaving it up to Brian. It was just easier than trying to protest.

In hindsight, perhaps Stephen should have protested more. This is often the case. People often regret not protesting things and most don't regret protesting things. I would suggest that you give protesting a go, at least once. You never know what you might end up making better. And, unless you're irrational or evil, I assume that making things better is right up your street. If nothing else, it would save me the bother.

As seemed to be the trend, upon Stephen's arrival at the meeting, he was greeted by more people than the week before. Most of these people had names of some kind, others had names of another kind and I'm not sure about the other others. It was getting more and more difficult for me to remember them, let alone for Stephen to remember them.

Once again, Brian took it upon himself to introduce Stephen to the group and he gave out the pamphlets to the new people that hadn't been there last week. He was very welcoming and kind and he was manipulating some very open and friendly arm gestures. Stephen felt slightly sick.

The meeting started as normal, a small discussion of some of the things we should do to be good people followed by some vague questions. It wasn't until about twenty minutes in to the meeting that something bizarre began happening.

'Stephen and I thought that this week we'd open up things a little bit more. Make sure you're all keeping an open mind and just letting the creativity and the unsolved mysteries of this universe wash over you. Because this mystery is what keeps us searching, y'know? And we must be careful of this mystery, y'know what I'm saying? What if we discover too much? Where would it all go?' A few people began nodding in agreement around the room. Stephen's feeling of feeling slightly sick worsened but he knew by now, more than ever, there was very little he could do.

'I have thought of a way to express this. Stephen helped me a lot in the first meeting we had. He encouraged me to get back into my writing and I've found it to be really helpful lately. I've been working on some bigger things and this is a little something I have managed to cobble together. It's just a story that, I feel, puts a lot of the ideas we've been discussing here into perspective. It just sort of came to me and I'd really like to take this opportunity to share it with you.' They all nodded with intrigue. Stephen took a sip of water to disguise his general bewilderment at what was happening as Brian began telling his story.

'This is the story of The Platinum Staircase,' began Brian.

Chapter 21

The Platinum Staircase

'This story is of a man named Ned. He lived in an ordinary enough house with an ordinary enough family in an ordinary enough street. But the adventure that he would embark upon would be as far from ordinary as one can go. Ned had often felt a certain gap in his life. It was hard to place exactly what it was but now and again it would deeply trouble him. If you have a gap in your wall then you call a builder but what about a gap in your essence? He would spend hours trying to establish what this gap actually was. He knew that only he could answer the mystery of the missing gap and only then could he set about rectifying the situation.

'One evening he was sitting alone in his living room listening to music and thinking to himself, "What is it? What am I missing?" It was then that he realised the magnitude of the hole. The gap that seemed relatively small a lot of the time was actually the biggest gap imaginable. Ned was searching for the truth, searching for the answer, searching for the *reason* for existence. He knew that this was not going to be an easy gap to fill. But he also knew that he needed to fill it if he was to go on with his life.

'It began to consume Ned. This was the most important idea that he'd ever thought about. He couldn't sleep for thinking about the vital need he had for filling this gap with the truth he sought. Ned had always been taught that if there is a problem then there is a solution to be found somewhere and so he decided that the only way to find this truth was to search the globe. For, "the answer must lie somewhere," he thought.

'He bade farewell to his family and began his search. He would talk to people, he would go into museums and he would spend days at a time alone in fields simply looking at the sky. His journey took him far and wide, he found himself travelling through every continent in the world, searching for that missing piece that would make his life complete. He was soon to be greeted by the answer to his search.

'One day, he was walking through the backstreets of either an Eastern European town or a Western Central American town and he came across a man draped in a black cloak. From this shadow of a man came a rasping voice that ordered him to stop. Ned was frightened at first but his fear was soon to vanish and be replaced with wonder. The voice came out of the shadows again and said:

'"You are a man who seeks the truth, I see." Ned was shocked beyond belief that the man had guessed such a thing and then he realised that the man wasn't guessing. He knew.

"Well, do you truly seek it?"

"Yes!" replied Ned with compelling enthusiasm. "More than anything, because it is everything. Everything else is nothing in comparison."

"Very well," said the darkness. "I feel you are worthy to hear of The Platinum Staircase."

And the void told him the tale of this amazing spectacle, he told him of how it reached higher than the clouds and higher still. He told him of its shimmering surface and the single door that it held on the top step. He told him of how running up it does not tire a person but only spurs them further with every step. He told him of how important it was to continue his search so as to fulfil his destiny. Ned stood with a gaping mouth as the tale was being told to him. He was enthralled and desperate and yearning to make his way towards this Staircase. The man could not tell him where it was but instead promised him that if he truly sought it, he would find it. And, very swiftly, the man disappeared back into the darkness that he had come from.

'Ned continued to travel the world. He knew that he hadn't physically made any more progress but, now that he knew what he was looking for, the task ahead seemed an easier one. His labouring search for ultimate truth was injected with a new level of excitement and everything The Platinum Staircase promised him pulled him forwards in his journey. For, at the top of the Staircase, there is a door and through the door is the answer to all of this mystery. No frilly bits, no room for interpretation, manipulation or alteration. On the other side of that door is unadulterated, absolute and eternal truth.

'On his travels he saw many amazing things. He witnessed spectacles beyond his wildest dreams but these things became more and more tiresome as his search for The Platinum Staircase dragged on and on and took him further and further around the world.

'One evening, he found himself in either a North African village or a in a mountain range in Western Asia. Ned laid his mind to rest in the corner of a shed he had stumbled across and sneaked into. He quickly drifted off to sleep and found himself deep in a darkened jungle. The noise of scuttling insects and nocturnal creatures pierced his ears as he slowly trudged through the marshy ground. He seemed to be tiptoeing, as though he was afraid to wake anything up. He didn't want to wake anything that he might frighten but, more importantly, anything that might frighten him.

'Suddenly, and without warning, the moon appeared before him in a gap in the trees and it provided him with light. He could now see the jungle that surrounded him, the darkness slowly faded and his eyes adjusted to the moonlight. Trees sprouted at random junctures through the jungle floor, layer upon layer of plant crept along one another's surface, fighting their way towards the sky. He could begin to see the insects scuttling, moving away from the parts of the trees that he was using to help him make his way through this alien landscape. He knew that this jungle was somehow otherworldly; it was a jungle but it was far from any kind of jungle he'd previously encountered on his journey around the world. Soon he could see the trees clearing ahead of him. At first it looked as though it were just his walking that was getting him to the clearing but he soon realised that the jungle itself was actually clearing. It was bending and folding and moving and parting and creating a pathway out onto a dusty road and there, deep in his mind, and beyond his belief, he saw that he had found the Staircase. He had been searching for decades across the world but here it lay inside his mind. It was beyond beautiful. Its first steps lay perfectly in front of him and each step was a very slight rotation on the last meaning that it slowly spiralled upwards towards the stars. He looked up and saw the staircase glimmering in the moonlight, and he could see it (or, rather, he couldn't see it) disappear beyond his sight into the night sky. It had no banister, but each step was wide and inviting. The first thing he did was place his palm onto its surface. It was cold, but reassuringly so. It was smooth. It was beyond beautiful.

'He was just as tired as he was in the physical world and he felt broken and weakened but before him he saw the Staircase shimmering and he found a sudden lease of life. His strength returned, he ignored his thirst and his hunger and he started running up the stairs. He was bounding, faster and faster, taking the steps two, three, four at a time. He felt the comforting stability of the platinum stairs beneath him as he continued pushing off them and reaching higher and higher. He ran for so long that hours became weeks became months. But time did not matter in this place.

'The stairs began to spiral more quickly; he followed them spiralling upwards and upwards until before him he could see the door. It looked a little out of place on top of the staircase. It was wooden and uninteresting but it was there in front of his eyes. He had made it. Absolute truth lay in front of him, just the other side of the door. He reached out his hand and began to force pressure down his arms to his fingertips. At the last millisecond he violently stopped himself.

'He couldn't do it. He could not push open the door. Nothing was stopping him but himself and he couldn't do it. It was just so defining. He couldn't cope with that kind of truth while he still wanted to live. He knew this now. It took truth to be on the other side of a door for him to realise this. One cannot be both living and all knowing.'

'Just think about it,' said Brian. 'Absolute truth. He had searched and searched. He had wanted this answer but, when the time came, he couldn't push open that door to find out. He didn't want to know. At least, not yet. He knew deep down that we are not ready until the time truly comes when we breathe our last breath. But then he felt that gap slowly fill, deep inside him. The idea that absolute truth could be laid in front of him but that he could decide that he wasn't ready was enough to create a level of fulfilment that he had never known before. He descended The Platinum Staircase and he slowly made his way back to the physical world.

'He awoke in a shed. He knew that he had really been there, though. It was the most real dream anyone could possibly have. It was hardly a dream at all. And he knew that he had done the right thing.'

A silence hung.

People were wide-eyed and shocked. Stephen took several more sips of water. Slowly, there grew a wave of clapping. Some people were genuinely impressed by Brian and his story, others were clapping because they'd heard clapping. He stood accepting the praise very openly. He mocked a dramatic bow. Everyone continued to clap for a little longer so that Stephen realised that this was actually full and genuine clapping, rather than the sarcastic one he had hoped for. Once again, looking around the room, the normally powerless Stephen realised that his normal state was entirely relevant now; he was completely and utterly powerless.

Stephen traipsed home from the meeting, resolving that he wouldn't be going back to one again. He felt guilty. He felt dirty all over, in fact. He decided to take a hot shower. He scrubbed violently with a sponge until it actually started to hurt a little bit, so he stopped.

After getting out of the shower, he proceeded to take the longest time getting dressed he'd ever known. Every attempt at putting his leg into his trousers seemed to fail. His mind was elsewhere. It was certainly not in a place concerned with the correct application of a pair of trousers.

He eventually got them on and went downstairs. For a while he just stood there with a blank look on his face. He didn't know whether he was going to go into the living room or the kitchen. He couldn't decide and so, through little fault of his own, he found himself walking in the park.

He sat on his bench. It was the same spot where he usually brought Elijah to set him free onto the grass to chase the wind. He had forgotten to bring Elijah this time and he hadn't taken a book, either. He just sat and thought while watching the trees move. I'm about to take you into his mind for a prolonged measure of time. Please do not become distressed, you are still you.

Here we go. Stephen was thinking about a lot of things but most of his thoughts were glazed with a painful, shameful guilt. I don't think that we really tend to think in sentences and Stephen's thoughts were definitely just a muddle of ideas brewing crazily around his brain matter. If I were to try and articulate them, they would be something like this:

'What have I done? Why did I create this? Should I keep going? Should I try to stop this? People can make up their own minds, can't they? I'm sure they'll soon see it for what it has become, won't they? I don't really want to use the word but is this a cult? Is that what this is now? Did I start a cult? No. No, surely I can't have. Could people be that ignorant and foolish? No, people are much cleverer than people give people credit for.'

Admittedly, even with my attempted articulation, it was clearly very haphazard in there. Or rather, it wasn't clearly haphazard, it was haphazardly haphazard. I'm sure you'll agree, though, that Stephen is asking himself a lot of questions and struggling to produce very clear answers. He's clearly in a lot of distress. Or rather, he is distressfully in a lot of distress. Just as he was hoping that he would have someone to talk to about this, preferably someone that he knows he can talk to, Wendy showed up.

'Hi, Stephen,' said Wendy. 'I thought you might be here. How's it going?'

'Not so great to be perfectly honest, Wendy. I've inadvertently created a cult.'

'Oh. That is a bad day. Today, I made a huge mistake on an order then I half-blamed someone else in a moment of panic and they got fully blamed for it and almost lost their job. And then I had to own up to it and I almost lost my job, until they realised I'm reasonably alright at what I do.' Just as she was uttering these words, a dog walked behind the bench and then moved out of visibility down an alley on the other side of the park. Wendy, however, didn't notice this and continued talking. 'Afterwards, they told me that they wished Sharon had done it because they'd wanted to fire her for a little while. I told them that that was a bit mean. They told me to "watch it" because they could still fire me. Anyway, back to your meetings. Do you know what my advice is? Stop going down there, it's only making it worse. You're upset every time you come back from one of those meetings. It's not your fault that this all got out of hand. Sometimes people just need something like this to feel safe. What happened today to prompt you to use the word "cult"?'

'They're living by "rules" for their lives. They've started making up stories and partially believing them.'

'Yep. Sounds like a cult to me. Well you've got to get out of there, Stephen.'

'You're right.'

'What happened to, "right you are"?' she said. This cheered Stephen up because of its ridiculous foolishness for at least a second or two and he concluded that he felt slightly better. He also concluded that he would never go back to that place. He was done with the 'Just Some Thoughts On How We Should Live Our Lives' pamphlet and 'The Platinum Staircase' and 'The Island' and anything else that was sprouting out of this. He would simply get on with his life and keep on track with his house being rebuilt. The house was being rebuilt, by the way, if you were worried. Just very, very slowly. This was not the fault of the builders, it was rather the fault of the fact that sorting out a burnt down house is quite a tricky business. I won't go into the details because it would take almost as long as actually doing it.

Stephen and Wendy wandered home at a leisurely pace to have some tea and watch some TV and have what most people like to call, 'a quiet night in'. However, while that's going I just want to turn back time a little bit (which I can do, by the way). This is just so that I can inform you of an event that was occurring at the same sort of time as Stephen and Wendy's bench discussion. At first it doesn't seem like a particularly exceptional event but its importance will become apparent soon enough.

Elijah had become quite taken by the idea of taking a small walk of his own in between his people-based walks. At the moment that Stephen and Wendy were just arriving home, he was also just arriving home from another of his pseudo-adventures. I shall inform you of how this pseudo-adventure went. He had raised his front legs to the handle of Wendy's side gate once again and watched it swing open before him. The darkening sky that could be seen through the alley down the side of Wendy's house beckoned Elijah forward as he made his way onto the street once more. He decided he wanted to take a different walk from last time but rational thought works in strange ways and, as he didn't even have rational thought, he ended up taking the same walk as the last time he was alone. He was strangely drawn to the house where he had heard the bizarre musings escape from the partially open window. This strange attraction may cause some people to assume some kind of cosmic connection or some kind of fate that is drawing the lives of Elijah and the man in the house (who I'm sure you have figured out is Brian) together. However, it's possibly a little more likely to be based on the intriguing smell of the urine on a lamppost near the house. He followed the trail of urine; some was his own, some belonged to other animals and some was the smell he sought.

He walked behind a bench in a park which held two people sitting. One of them was telling a story about a mess up with an order. He recognised them but he was very busy. He continued walking towards the alley he had taken the last time that he had gone for his walk.

He continued his sniffing-related adventure until he was back on the street and standing next to the lamppost he was so intrigued by. At the exact moment that he was standing there, a woman and a man in a nearby window, who had previously been talking between themselves, were looking at a dog. They soon returned to their discussion and, if Elijah was able to understand English, he would have resolved that the following was said:

'You need to find out where he works. You need to bump into him, somehow.'

'How?'

'I don't care how. Just find out. We need to find out where he stands on this subject because, if he's slipping the way it seems that he is, then we're going to have a big problem on our hands. We need the smooth transition from just having some people around to actually having paying customers to be just that; smooth.'

'Okay. Okay. I already know all of this. Why are you going into so much detail? It seems as if you're trying to pass on as much information as possible in a very short period of time.'

'Never mind that. Just make sure he's coming to the next meeting with the right mindset. He seems to have taken something of a liking to you. I'll try and defuse the situation if it gets out of hand but if he is comfortable and is able to approach me separately then maybe he'll be interested in joining in the profits.'

'And if he isn't?'

'Then we'll have to find a way of dealing with that.'

If Elijah understood the concept of spoken language and also understood English and had a similar field of perception to a human then there would have been a slight possibility that he might have understood the dramatic nature of Brian's closing sentence. But he didn't; so he didn't. Instead, he decided that he'd reached the saturation of sniffing urine that he was happy with and so headed back towards Wendy's house.

By the time he got back to the park, there was no one at the bench but he gave it a sniff to confirm that he had definitely recognised the people who had sat there earlier. He then bounded back towards the side gate of Wendy's house and made his way into her back garden. Once again, he had been and gone without detection and he welcomed every pat on the head with extreme enthusiasm.

Chapter 22

Hanky On A Stick

The funny thing about decisions is that, even if one makes one, it might not always be the decision one wishes one had made. To give an example, I will use the decision of whether you want to go on a bicycle ride or a scooter ride. This will lead you to do one of two things, depending on what kind of person you are.

One option is to just make the decision without thought. This would be by detaching yourself from any sort of over-complicated, rational analysis and just pointing at, say, the scooter. This will probably mean you'll be happy enough with your decision because you did not think it through too much and didn't give yourself things to worry about on your pleasant scooter ride.

The other way of going about making your decision is by trying to think it through rationally. Each person will have their own personal rationale for this decision. For example, one person might think, 'Well, I've never ridden a scooter before, I'll try that out.' Another person might think, 'Well,

I've never ridden a scooter before, I'd better take the bike.' By this, I mean that rational thought can be subjective a lot of the time. So, even though we pride ourselves on being very rational creatures (which we no doubt are compared to, say, the moth), we can sometimes use our rational thought in weird and wonderful ways. We can use it to justify a decision that we've made deep down, without really knowing why we've made that decision.

Sometimes rationality is instinct's slave. I'm not knocking it, though. It's better than anything I've ever managed to do. And for another matter (and this may shock you), I don't know what I'm talking about. And for another, another matter, I must press on with Stephen's story; it really is very important.

Don't worry, that last train of thought was not completely irrelevant. It is vaguely related to Stephen's thought-process as he sat, with his mind wandering, at his desk at work. 'I definitely won't go to the next meeting,' was the last thing that Stephen thought before he went to bed the night before. But now, he was sitting at his desk, squeezing a stress ball quite violently and wondering whether he was making the correct decision. Here, we can see how an entire thought process can get you to the decision you really want, despite there being a rational argument on both sides:

'Wendy's right. I definitely shouldn't go. The meetings only make me distressed and upset. Those people have given in to

Brian and his take-over tactics. And if they have then that's their problem. It's not up to me to teach people or to try to change people or to have anything to do with the way people think, I've got my own muddled brain to deal with.

But then again, I feel somewhat responsible for this. I did start it. Those people need my help. Brian is clearly somewhat disturbed; *he* needs my help. I seem to be the only one that can see this for what it is becoming and I'm the only one that can possibly do anything about it. One could almost say that it is my responsibility to go to that meeting and tell them what is going on. I definitely have to go. Wendy's wrong.'

I think you'll agree that 'Wendy's right' and 'Wendy's wrong' are the antithesis of one another, yet Stephen's rational thinking has led him to this conclusion. Believe me, I am not knocking rational thought. It's fantastic. It's just that sometimes I'm at the bottom of a hill and I realise that I probably should have come on the bike.

While taking his lunch break from work, Stephen was walking towards one of the large variety of filled baguette outlets near his office when he bumped into someone that made him struggle to speak. His manner suddenly altered from an adult person with a job who eats baguettes for lunch into a teenage boy as he looked into Flo's eyes. Her eyes forced their way into his somehow. She seemed to be looking at the inner-workings of his mind. He felt exposed.

'Hello,' she said, rather traditionally. She was wearing a blouse and long skirt. It became apparent that she was probably on her lunch break from work as well. Stephen decided that there was something to talk about there and that this was beyond the perfect opportunity.

'Hi. Are you on lunch, too?'

'Yeah. What a morning!' she said. 'You fancy going somewhere for lunch?' She finished the situation off for him, which was lucky because he wasn't totally certain that he could carry it through to its logical conclusion on his own.

He found it difficult to retain an air of calm as he said, 'Yes! Definitely! Let's go!' As you can see, he found it very difficult indeed.

It was not long before they found themselves sitting in an unimaginative baguette dispenser surrounded by pictures of baguettes that looked nothing like the ones they were eating. Stephen was explaining his problems with the group and Flo was taking on the character of someone who was agreeing with him.

'It's just that it's never what I intended, you know? It's all got a bit… weird.'

'I think you're right. If you don't mind me saying, it's all got a bit…'

'Culty?' offered Stephen.

'Exactly,' said Flo through a mouth filled with bread and questionable chicken.

And so this went on. They talked past the time they should have both gone back to work. He continued to look at her and was amazed by every movement she made and every word that came out of her questionable-chicken-filled mouth. They suddenly realised the time when they looked around to find the café empty besides themselves. Just as they were grabbing their things together to head back to work, Flo suddenly turned to Stephen and grabbed his arm.

'Can I offer you some advice?'

'Sure.'

'I think you need to go back there one more time. You'll regret it forever if you don't. You need to chat to Brian. Maybe this is all a big misunderstanding with crossed wires. There's a chance you can still work together to do something good. To do something to help those people.'

Stephen felt as though she had known him for years. She had got into his mind and set up a little home or another more effective metaphor.

Decisions that appear to be based on rationality can often be based on something that someone you're infatuated with told you to do. Stephen would do anything to please Flo and that is why he was completely resolved to ignore Wendy's advice.

The sun rose over a Thursday horizon. Stephen spent much of his day at his desk, pretending to work but actually planning how he was likely to act at the next meeting. He would be civil and try to talk things over with Brian. He would do what Flo said. Obviously.

Once Friday evening had made itself known fully, Stephen began making his way around to the community centre. He continued to say civil things in his head like 'Hello' and 'How are you?' and various sentences like that. He was most certainly familiar with acting this way as it was the way he had constantly acted throughout his life.

But once he was in there and witnessing all of the usual proceedings taking place he realised how difficult all of this was. Brian would refer back to his Platinum Staircase story and people would begin offering their personal meaning to it and how it had helped them to realise some things. Others were stating how they had felt the same thing for years but had felt a happiness wash through them since they had thought about it fully. Some began expressing how they felt just like Ned and they know just why he did what he did. Stephen began to feel lost in a sea of general silliness.

Stephen's decision to remain civil became a little more tested with each new proclamation of a rediscovered happiness or an insistence that truth was not something that could be seen but that it was something that is felt. And very suddenly, without much warning from Stephen's brain, his mouth began to bellow something that was directed towards Brian. This was certainly something unfamiliar to everyone present, as well as to Stephen. The hall was filled with enough people to fill a double-decker bus and have three people standing at the bottom of the stairs, discussing something partially humorous that their friend did when he was inebriated last night. But, despite the presence of all of these people, Stephen's voice managed to force all of their voices into silence as his rang out through the hall.

'Right. I'm not even here!' and he stood up.

This confused Brian, somewhat. It confused everyone, including me, in fact. Stephen was immediately disappointed. The speech he had briefly prepared in his head had just been thoroughly ruined by himself and his confusing opening statement. The air of authority that he had hoped to maintain flew very suddenly out of a window, which was also strange because all the windows were closed.

'Um… I think you'll find you *are* here, Stevey.' Stephen had now entered a further layer of confusion as he was now entrenched in some kind of discussion about existence with Brian. Stephen was almost definitely certain that he was there and so, he would therefore have to agree with Brian on this one. But he wasn't really in the mood for agreement so, rather than the usually affirmative 'Yes' that denotes agreement, he opted for the opposite.

'No, no. What I mean is, I'm not here in the sense that I want to be here. I'm not here in the sense that I've come down here for a meeting. I am merely here in the sense that I don't want to be here and that I just knew this is where you'd be and I needed to talk to you.'

Brian stood, open-mouthed, in confusion but then decided the best conclusion was just to invite Stephen back to his seat.

'Well, maybe it'd be best if you came and sat back down and we can discuss this without shouting,' was the way he went about inviting him back to his seat.

Stephen was about to give in to his instincts, he was just about to listen to Brian, when he remembered why he was there.

'No. Wait. I came here to talk to you. I came to talk to all of you but particularly to Brian.'

There was a silence that washed around the hall now, a silence stronger than Stephen's original interruption caused. They realised fully that Stephen seemed to be very serious and angry. They had never seen Stephen serious or angry before, certainly not both at the same time, and this made many of them become serious themselves. It made one person angry but that person had issues with anger that he was trying to resolve.

'Brian,' said Stephen, seeming far too comfortable with the silence, it was all very out of character, 'I just want to ask you, can't you see what this has become?'

'What do you mean Stevey-boy? Come on, out with it. We're all friends here.'

'This, Brian, is turning into a cult.'

'What?'

'I've created a cult, Brian!'

People around the room were reacting differently to all of this drama. Some were in confused awe, the classic wide-eyed and wide-mouthed look that doesn't tend to happen in real life was occurring for some people. Most, however, were looking down and trying to avoid the whole situation. They escaped inside their own heads and became really interested by pieces of fluff on their trousers or the best way to cross one's arms. You will also notice that Stephen is saying 'Brian' quite a lot as people tend to do when they're angry with someone. I don't mean that they would just say, 'Brian'; the name depends on the person they are actually angry at. This is, of course, if they decide to choose rage (that is a reference from very long ago, possibly as far as Chapter 2. I wouldn't worry about it too much). Brian tried to remain calm in the hope that Stephen would join him,

'Now, Stevey-boy, let's just all calm down. One thing is for sure: this is not a cult. We're just talking here, openly chatting, just the way you like it. There's a small fee and then everyone is allowed to contribute...' He was suddenly interrupted.

'A fee?' demanded Stephen. 'You're charging a fee? When did this start?'

'Oh. It's just to cover expenses. Nothing major. Just because the more of these lovely people that show up, the more expensive it becomes to keep it all running.'

'What are you talking about? What expenses?' But Stephen realised that now was not the time to get side-tracked by this new information so he returned instead to the matter at hand.

'Do you know what I came here to say? I came to tell you that you're just a coward, Brian. You know that? You couldn't handle it when you left your religion. It was so safe, so secure, which I understand fully. But you couldn't handle it and you've placed your belief elsewhere. And now you've gone drunk on power. Power that you made up in the first place.'

'Can I just stop you there, Stephen? You've become a little hysterical. You're blowing things a little out of proportion. I don't think all the people that keep coming back in greater numbers each week would agree with you. They simply see this as a place of solitude. A place where they can let out any of their problems without having to fork out ridiculous prices on a psychiatrist or a counsellor or something. We're just a much cheaper alternative that is providing a kind service,' concluded Brian. This seemed to make most people in the hall happy. It didn't make Stephen very happy, of course.

'Now, Stephen. I think that the good people here might have had enough of this shouting. They can think for themselves, and that's why they choose to come here. I'm sensing a lot of hatred from you, Stephen. I would like to refer you and everyone else to page 5 of your pamphlets. Don't we all agree that Stephen may be showing some unnecessary hatred towards our beliefs and our thoughts and our general decisions? I mean, you interpret that as you wish but I think that that is definitely what Stephen is doing right now. I hate to do this, but I think maybe you just need to take some time to think things through. It would probably be best if we asked you to leave. If you have simply come here to shout at us and don't want to contribute, then I think it's for the best.'

'I will. I am most certainly leaving.' He stumbled over these last words as he pushed open the doors that led to the darkening corridor and eventually outside.

He was breathing really quite heavily now and his blood was pumping very quickly. He was not used to such a bombardment of anger, confrontation and prolonged and fixed attention all at once. He wasn't sure whether he liked it. He also started to worry about himself. He even questioned his own sanity. He wasn't sure whether Brian might have been right. Was he blowing this all out of proportion? Was he overreacting? Was he seeing something that wasn't really there? Maybe a small fee is necessary. But the fact that Brian had actually managed to turn Stephen's own thoughts on him annoyed Stephen even more as he made the short trip back towards Wendy's house. If he didn't know any better, he would have said he was stomping.

I can't recall exactly what Brian said after Stephen left the meeting but I'm sure he would have calmed everyone down. And he would have found a way to steer everyone back towards the conversation they were having about The Island and The Platinum Staircase and about the recruitment scheme they were soon employing to try and help more lost people who might want to find solace in their gatherings. He may have also explained that Stephen wasn't quite as angry as he seemed to be, he was simply going through a lot lately. He may even have referred to the fact that he had recently enjoyed a conversation with Stephen about The Platinum Staircase and that the only reason the idea was beginning to be too much for him to handle was because it resonated with something deep inside him. Brian may have explained that Stephen felt a deep connection with the concept, something that he had never felt before. Some words had started to leak out of him, words that were out of his control but that he could see in the hazy distance. These words were 'Love', 'Peace', 'Happiness' and 'Goldfish'. Brian explained that Stephen couldn't say any more than that but Stephen had told him that he felt that their significance would become apparent soon.

Stephen found himself walking home much quicker than any natural rate, half-stomping his way up the hill towards Wendy's house. He had never felt so many things that he couldn't describe all at once, let alone even attempting to describe what they all felt like together, so I am certainly not going to try and explain it. He felt it best not to think too much about it, which was convenient for me. He'd try and bottle it up like he always did. At least, until he discussed it in depth with Wendy in the park the next day.

Chapter 23

The Size Of Rubies

Stephen would best be described as 'in despair'. The reason he would best be described as 'in despair' is because he was very much in despair. He sat at Wendy's house in an armchair looking at nothing and trying to think about nothing but not really being able to.

Now you may think this is all a bit overly dramatic (and so did I until I thought about it) but if Stephen's right and these people do end up as some kind of deluded cult then he can't help but feel somewhat responsible and he can't help but worry about their welfare.

Did he stand up against it enough? Did he protest enough? These are some of the questions he was asking. Perhaps you would answer both of these with 'No' (and so did I until I thought about it) but Stephen obviously didn't have the benefit of hindsight at the time. Of course he didn't, that's the whole point of hindsight; if we had the benefit of hindsight at the time then we'd all be making perfect decisions and be able to think through the different options. But then it would all get very complicated as different people made interrelated decisions. And, if people were constantly using their hindsight to monitor the present, what sort of life would that be? In hindsight, a world where we could have constant hindsight would be awful.

So there Stephen sat, with the benefit of hindsight on the situation (which he didn't see as much of a benefit, rather a torture) wondering whether there was anything more he could do. It came to the point where he had officially, 100%, entirely, absolutely and totally given up on the whole situation. So, he turned on the TV and watched the Lottery. As the numbers came up he wished he always had the benefit of hindsight.

Wendy arrived home, wandered into the living room and saw Stephen looking somewhat distressed.

'Hey there, soldier. What's up?'

'"What's up?" doesn't really suit you, did you know that?'

'I know, yeah, I'm sorry. I was just trying something out. How about, what's wrong?'

'And the "soldier" was a bit odd.'

'Yeah, sorry about that, too. Anyway, what's going on?'

'That's a bit extreme,' said Stephen, 'sounds like you've just wandered in during a bloody brawl.'

'Oh, just answer the question, Stephen.'

'Sorry. Oh, y'know, the usual.'

'Grab your coat; I think it's best to go where we go at times like these. It's a good thing all of this is happening during such a good bout of weather, don't you think? It's never rained once as we think of heading over to…' but she had already gently closed the door before we could hear the end of this sentence.

And there they sat again, the bench being the place that Stephen felt most comfortable and, therefore, the most comfortable opening up to Wendy.

'It really, very definitely is a cult now, Wendy. I went there today, you should have heard him.' And off he went. He explained the events of Chapter 22 to Wendy, although he obviously didn't explain it as Chapter 22.

Stephen explained about Brian and the fact that he'd started charging money. He wondered where it was going. Not that he wanted any. He knew that he didn't want any; he saw what this was becoming. It was exploitation, the exploitation of a person's vulnerability to make some money. At the end of his tirade of meandering thoughts, Wendy took a second to appreciate a moment of silence before offering her words.

'Well, thanks for not listening to me, by the way, before I start offering advice,' said Wendy.

'I know. I'm sorry. It was a whole big bike and scooter incident.'

'I won't ask,' she said. 'Anyway, will you take my advice this time around?'

'Yeah. Well, actually, what is it?'

'It's exactly the same as my last piece of advice. Only this time I really, really mean it in the hope that you'll really, really listen to it. This is for your own sanity. And you know what, Stephen; if you don't listen to my advice this time around I will be very, very disappointed.'

Stephen felt it best to listen to the advice. No one needs disappointment from anyone, let alone disappointment prefixed by two 'really, really's and a 'very, very' from their only true friend.

They sat a little while longer on the bench. They decided to discuss something completely different from their usual topics and they did it with surprising ease. As the evening drew on, Stephen felt a lifting from inside his chest that travelled to his shoulders and then slowly departed into the sky. He identified it as worry. He witnessed his worry swimming off towards the sunset as they decided to turn back towards the place that Stephen had come to think of as home.

The trouble is that another scooter and bike issue came up, but not until Chapter 25. There's no rush, though, is there? I've got to include all the facts here. I'm just making sure you read the whole of Chapter 24. Everything is becoming very important indeed, perhaps the most important it has been so far, and I'm sure that you'll love to hear about what Stephen saw around the streets of his town about two weeks later.

Chapter 24

And The People All Stared Into Space

I t was a few weeks later. Two to be precise. So, it was actually a couple of weeks later but let's not get into semantics, I'm not one to travel off on tangents. Stephen was innocently wandering into town one weekend for, what he described to Wendy as, 'some bits'. It was one of those 'some bits' trips where the odd little errands all build up until one cannot avoid them any longer and one has to go and try and sort it all out so one can feel a little happier when one watches a film at night without feeling guilty about avoiding things one should be doing.

There aren't that many problems with life when you think about it. There is of course the impending threat of death, the possibility of illness, money worries, job worries, commitments to things we don't enjoy, conversations, the fear of war, the fear of pain, general fears that people have, the need to keep fit, the need to leave our mark in history, the need to try and keep on top of news and events from around the world, the worry of whether it's all worth it or whether we're making the most of our time here, the worry that we've not done enough to help our fellow humans, the worry that we've not done enough to help our fellow animals, the guilt felt when considering the millions suffering around the world, the apocalypse, the fear of offending people inadvertently, the need to try and gain knowledge as and when we can... but apart from these there isn't that much to worry about. However, as discussed at some other point, one of the problems that I find is that one is never in a state where everything is 'done', so to speak. There is never a time where one can sit and quite honestly say 'there is nothing I need to do'. The only time this is true is when one is a child but by the time one is about 14 years old, that will never be the case again. To counter that bleakness, perhaps it's best to consider that that's just the way it is, and that everyone's in the same boat, and let's just try and enjoy it, yeah?

Anyway, Stephen was making a futile attempt at getting to that state where he could say, 'I have nothing to do,' by heading into town for his 'bits'. These included bulbs, batteries, a word with the bank, some envelopes, and the beginnings of a discussion about getting a new mobile phone. But he was stopped in his tracks as he arrived on the main high-street. He had just been looking down at his list of things he had to pick up, and, after reading the word 'phone', he looked up to see a most horrifying sight.

This horrifying sight included banners. This horrifying sight included intrusive people. This horrifying sight included Brian. This horrifying sight made Stephen, without any control over his thought processes, immediately think of the word, 'minions'.

He carefully avoided them and decided to watch from the side of the street because, deep down, for some reason, people like to torture themselves just so that they can have something to moan about.

He caught small snippets of conversation through the passing crowds on the high-street. Everyone seemed to be going somewhere. This is because every single one of them had something to do and they will never be out of that state. I'm sorry, I'm becoming bleak again. Perhaps, if you had the organisational skills, you could arrange an event called 'Stop Day' that had one, maybe even two, exclamation marks. This day would be a day where everyone stopped doing those tasks that need doing and forgot about them for a bit and just read a book, for example. If you could organise it so that it was this book then that would really help me out. People need to hear about Stephen's story. It really is very important. If you could just get on with organising that while I carry on with the rest of this then that would be fantastic. Just put it on your list of things to do.

The people on the street were saying things like:

'Don't you find that sometimes you have fading feelings of happiness? No? Okay, thanks for your time.'

'The main thing that we long for is some kind of direction, don't you find? Yes? You'd agree with me, yeah? What we do is very simple indeed…'

'Yeah. It's just an hour's meeting every Friday at the moment but we're hoping this expands if enough funds are available.'

'No? Not interested? Thank you for your time, anyway.'

And, perhaps worst of all, 'Yes. It's the story of The Platinum Staircase.'

He was moving with military efficiency between bins and phone-boxes so as to avoid detection when he heard a voice over his shoulder. He turned in trepidation but was relieved to see that it was aimed at someone else. He was walking away when he heard what they were saying. 'No. That's fine. You can keep that pamphlet. As it says on the front, it really is "Just Some Thoughts". If you change your mind then come along next week. We won't bite!'

Stephen had to continue his military operation to avoid detection for even longer as he rounded the corner to see yet more people. Everyone's smile was disgustingly, excessively wide. The banners were worse. They said things like:

UNHAPPY? ASK US HOW WE CAN HELP!

WE ALL NEED DIRECTION.

MYSTERY MAKES US HUMAN. MYSTERY
KEEPS US ALIVE.

They were recruiting and they were merry both at exactly the same time, making Stephen's guilt rise from his stomach and settle somewhere around his throat.

Stephen was almost entirely put off getting his 'bits' on the high-street now. If he didn't have his list to refer to, he would have forgotten every single one in that moment. He persevered, however. I am not suggesting that this was some brave act; I am just suggesting that that is exactly what he did. He surreptitiously sneaked between the different shops that he needed to travel to and was not once spotted by anyone holding a banner.

After a successfully stealthy shopping trip, he made his way back home to make a decision on whether he should take any further action after seeing this. He was in a situation where he wasn't sure what decision he actually wanted as the outcome, so he decided to just go for one and then see if he would rationally try and change it to the other one. His thought process, which I'm sure you are probably getting quite familiar with by now, went something like this:

I said I wouldn't get involved. This is for my own sanity. I should listen to Wendy this time.

But this is all getting very out of hand.

And I don't have to go to a meeting again, just as I promised Wendy. I could just go to Brian's house and confront him alone.

He's started charging and now he's recruiting on the street, this can only lead to a bad place.

Maybe I could make a promise to myself that this is my final stab, my final chance at doing something.

It is my duty to do something.

If I don't then I'm going to go insane.

I need to get involved for my sanity. I should ignore Wendy again.

And so, even though Stephen had initially thought he wanted to go by bike, he ended up rationalising that a scooter was the better option (see some other chapter). Oddly, however, he went home on the bus which just threw something else into the mix that he couldn't convincingly fit into the metaphor.

After the short bus trip, where he thought of very little at all, he got off at his stop and remembered, very suddenly, the decision that he had rationally decided upon. He added to this rational decision by rationally deciding that he would go to Brian's house tomorrow, after finding out exactly where it is.

Chapter 25

And So She Walked On Her Feet Instead

One way or another, Stephen found out exactly where Brian lived. I don't want to go into too many details because I can't afford to lose you now. I'm almost certain that it involved phoning him up and asking directions to his house. We're so close to finding out what happened to Stephen, I've got to keep you here to the end. By this I mean it is the farthest point you could come and be allowed to give up. I am not normally the kind to force people into things, I tend to be of the opinion that the things that people do are up to the people that do those things. That's just common sense. But I'm afraid, without being too forceful, I will not allow you to leave now. This is far too important.

Stephen made his way around to Brian's house which turned out to be on the other side of the park. No wonder he would meet him there so often. Shortly after passing through the park, he was directly in front of Brian's house. Shortly after being directly in front of Brian's house, he was ringing his door bell.

Brian opened it reasonably promptly, he had his usual cigarette slowly burning in his mouth and he somehow managed to cultivate a look that was both shocked and welcoming at exactly the same time.

'Stevey-boy!' he said, somewhat more hesitantly than he would normally but still with a decent amount of unnecessary enthusiasm. 'Come on in! How're things?'

This was all too pleasant for Stephen's liking. He had come to confront Brian in a way that he'd never been used to and he ended up just exchanging his tired, old pleasantries that get him nowhere.

Stephen was, without much warning from his brain, in Brian's hallway. He didn't know where he was going to begin. He'd already tried confronting Brian with sense and reason which was of little success, if any at all. But a phrase returned to Stephen that he'd never been able to fully utilise until this moment. It was, 'Desperate times call for desperate measures.' But before Stephen had any time to think it through anymore, Brian had said,

'Cup of tea or coffee or something?'

'Actually, yeah. I'll take a cup of tea if you're offering.'

'I am indeed offering. One cup of tea coming up. Just head into the living room there,' he gestured towards the first room on Stephen's right, 'and make yourself at home.'

Stephen decided this meant something along the lines of, 'sit down somewhere and act comfortable,' and so he did. After sitting for a while and acting comfortable, Brian returned with the tea. As he rounded the corner into the living room, he began speaking with his mouth,

'So, Stephen,' began Brian, 'what brings you here?'

'I was beginning to wonder myself,' said Stephen as if he was some kind of a ridiculous person in a ridiculous film. He would have apologised for that but it was already too late so he just decided to move on. 'I was just wondering whether you'd considered some of the things I'd said when I got a bit agitated the other week at the meeting.' He took a sip of tea and did not seem at all apologetic about getting agitated. This was because he wasn't.

'Um… Yeah,' was Brian's conclusion to a very quick period of thought, 'I considered them in a way. But I must say that I still disagree with most, if not all, of what you said.'

Stephen tried his best to continue to remain calm. He sipped his tea very quickly and hid his face behind the mug and, as a consequence, scalded the roof of his mouth. He felt it best not to bring that up right now. Again, he just moved on.

'Okay. That's fair enough. It's just that I feel very, very strongly about this indeed.'

'I am aware of that, Stephen, and I sympathise, but that isn't enough to convince me. If we altered our thoughts whenever we came across another person that had a strong opinion on something then we'd be flitting here and there all over the place, wouldn't we, now? Those people down there need that place, y'know? They need somewhere to go to talk through all of those issues. That's what I thought you wanted.'

'Yes. Yes, that's true. But you must understand that that is *all* I wanted. Nothing more than that. You've started to turn this into an organisation. You've started to make a profit. You're reaping the benefits of other people's vulnerable states. I certainly didn't want that.'

'Do you stand by that?'

'Definitely. I think what you're doing is disgraceful. You're not qualified. You're just taking people's money and giving them magic beans. And there's no such thing as magic beans.' Stephen very much wished he'd prepared this speech a little better. He was half way through saying 'magic beans' when he knew he couldn't back out. He had to see the metaphor through to the end, even though he had grown to hate it. I know a little how he feels.

'Well. Things change, y'know?' And that was it. That was finally it. There are only a certain number of times that people can hear 'y'know?' from one person within a certain period of time and withstand it. There is a very complicated mathematical formula that I don't understand that manages to squeeze in all the variables and produce an equation for this very situation. One very important variable in this situation was that Stephen was already reasonably angry. Another important variable was that Brian was a very smug person and said, 'y'know?' without even a hint of irony or sarcasm.

The mathematical formula that the researchers identified included the 'no-turning-back' point. This is the moment where the subject can no longer hear it without at least making a half-joking comment about it to raise the issue. However, there is the further 'no-turning-back' moment, which is the one Stephen was in, where a half-joking 'just thought I'd raise it' comment is very far out of reach. There is, rather, (according to the formula and a pinch of probability) a much more likely chance that there will be a very violent outburst involving a sarcastic repetition of the annoying person's name loudly in their face as if they had anything to do with its choosing. Stephen was most definitely at 'no-turning-back' point number two and it all came quickly, rapidly and violently flooding out. This is how it went:

'Well, *Brian*, I wouldn't want to stand in the way of progress, *Brian*. I wouldn't want to get in the way of your little power trip, *Brian*!' shouted Stephen. The shout was getting louder with each word and Stephen's salivating abilities were becoming more and more apparent with every syllable.

'Now, Stephen. I resent that. I am not on a power trip.'

'I could tell them all, you know,' said Stephen. This was the beginning of a threat.

'What?'

'I saw you yesterday, recruiting people to join your little cult. I know exactly what you're doing. I know where this began. Some people were there early on but only I know exactly what you've been up to since the very start. You're so confused, Brian. You need help. And I know this is a false service. I will tell them all what a sham it all is until it no longer exists. Some people are happy to be misled but, if this gains any kind of following, I'll go to the papers and I'll take it down bit by bit. I could turn you into a laughing stock. Because I know, *Brian*, I know who you really are. I seem to be the only one that does but I most certainly do. And I won't stop until you've been fully revealed for who you are. I will show them that this is all a front for something a lot more frightening.'

'I don't like being threatened, Stephen. It makes me a little nervous.'

'Well, I think that's the whole bloody point in threatening people, Brian. It tends to be to try to get the person a little bit nervous! And believe you me, you should be nervous because I'm not the person that stands by and watches things like this happening anymore. I used to be, but not anymore. I *will not* let this happen. I will do everything in my power to bring you guys down before it's too late.'

I will concede that things got a bit dramatic just then and Stephen embarrassed himself a little bit in that respect but I also think that we can all be proud of what he's bringing himself to do. We know it's not really in his nature and we know that he is resorting to desperate measures in these desperate times. It tends to be generally accepted that one often does not know how one will act in a given situation unless one is actually in that given situation. Stephen would be the first to admit that he is unlikely to try and interfere in most things, especially not things that have clearly grown out of his control. But Stephen seems to have come through in this instance. He has proven that people can sometimes prove themselves wrong.

'Stephen. Am I to take these threats seriously?'

'I'm afraid so. You've left me little choice.'

'Okay. Just so that I know where we stand on the issue.'

All of this is getting far too serious for my liking. I can only apologise again. This is exactly what happened and it pains me to show Stephen at such low points. I'm sure you will agree, however, that these desperate measures are quite just at this time.

But this all gets a bit lower and it all gets a bit darker because, now, another day comes around and it's another day of Stephen in the park, wondering about last night's events and where this all may lead. He was going to keep his word, though. He agreed with Brian that he would monitor what was happening at the meetings and then take further action if need be. He was being fair with his threats.

This day in the park smoothly ran into an evening at the park. The light was dimming and the clouds were beginning to grow much darker in the sky. Stephen was reading on the bench when there was a sudden flash in the distance and a slow and steady roll of thunder a second or two afterwards.

Not five seconds later did the clouds give up on holding any more water and the rain cascaded harshly and quickly from the sky above. What started out as a few drops on the pages of Stephen's book, causing him to close it suddenly, became rain pounding the cover loudly and forcing him to put it back into his bag. The rain was searing onto Stephen's face as he looked around to see what he thought was an empty park.

He was just getting up to go, when a figure approached him from behind the trees.

Chapter 26

Where No One Has Been Before

'I couldn't agree more, Stephen, because you have left me no choice.'

I'm attempting to do it again; it's another one of those chapters that starts in the middle. It feels like the right time in what can only be described as the climax of this story.

We left Chapter 25 at a very exciting time, the park was clearing of its last few people because of the sudden rainfall and alone in the park were Stephen and a figure who had appeared mysteriously from behind the trees.

I will inform you now, just to confirm the suspicions that many of you will have, the mysterious figure is, of course, Brian. He had digested what Stephen had said the day before and he'd taken some time to have a proper think about this whole situation. Suddenly something had hit him and he felt it best to go and speak to Stephen in a quiet, darkened place.

Just as Stephen was making his way onto the path and about to depart from the rainy park, he noticed the shadow approach him. He looked at it in fear, he stood rigid and was ready to run but for the first time that he could remember, he was relieved to see Brian.

'Oh, Jesus! Didn't see you there, Brian. You frightened me.'

Brian seemed unwavering in his emotion as he pretended to say, 'Sorry about that, Stevey.'

'Well. What brings you to the park this evening, just another quick walk?' Stephen was trying his best to break up this odd atmosphere that was being created by the driving rain and the rolling thunder and the strange expression on Brian's face with light-hearted chatter.

'Not exactly. I felt I needed to have another talk with you,' his voice remaining unsettlingly calm. Stephen tried to pick up the mood again.

'Okay. Well, shall we try and find some shelter somewhere, perhaps head to pub down the road or something…'

'No. Here will do just fine,' said Brian, his hair soaking and sticking to his forehead as the rain continued to pound on both of the men. Stephen was definitely confused by this response but something told him it was best not to argue at this time.

He'd seen similar fleeting moments in Brian's eyes but there was something different this time. Something irretrievable. 'So are you still sure that your threats are real?' said Brian, having to speak louder over some rumbling thunder. The rain was growing harsher and forcing both parties to squint against it.

The reason I know this is because a fork of lightning lit up Stephen's face as he said, 'I'm afraid so, Brian. I can't be the one that lets this sort of thing slide anymore. I will do everything in my power to stop you from doing the things you're doing to those people.'

'That was what I was afraid of,' said Brian. 'Do you realise how much I lost when I lost God, Stephen?'

Stephen was a bit taken aback by this; he hadn't expected this kind of conversation with Brian again.

'Um... well, I know you lost your... direction,' he offered.

'Don't mock me, Stephen!' said Brian, 'I lost so much more than that. I lost who I was. You see, I'm a believer.' Stephen resisted the unbelievable temptation to break into The Monkees' classic which had melted with all of the other 'M's in his CD collection. Instead, he kept his eyes glaring into Brian's and he felt Brian's glaring right back at him. 'I'm a person that can see beyond the world you live in.'

'But don't you see, Brian? Those are all just empty words. You're adding things to the world that aren't there. You can say and write lovely things that make you and the people around you feel better but it just makes you all become so confused. Happy, but confused.'

'And what's wrong with that?'

'I suppose there's nothing wrong in the sense that it's not physically harming anyone. But surely you want to see the real world in all its beauty. And surely there is harm in preying on the weaker, struggling ones to bring them to your side so that you can get some money and feel better about your fantastical beliefs.'

'Shut up!' said Brian, 'I am warning you, Stephen, I think it's best for you to well and truly shut up. You told me wonderful things in the first meeting. Things that affirmed my reason for existence. I want to write, I want people to read what I write. But, more than that, I want them to feel what I write and be affected deep inside.'

'You can still do that. There's nothing stopping you.'

'That's where you're wrong, Stephen. There is something stopping me. You're stopping me.'

The rain was getting heavier now, Stephen was positively dripping wet. He was beginning to shiver as the evening wind rushed through the pores of his clothing and grazed his skin.

'What do you mean?' asked Stephen with trepidation.

'I mean that I can go beyond simply making people think as they close the last page of a book. I have an opportunity before me that means I can get inside people's fundamental ideological outlook, I can write words that will alter the way they see the world around them. What can be more wonderful and empowering as a writer than that?'

'But don't you see how harmful that is? To alter someone so much?'

'No. I'm saving them. I've gone beyond simply writing about something. I *believe* in what I'm writing. And that way I can truly write what I feel. It's not enough to put on the act. I am truly writing to aid people. But you're the final ingredient, Stephen. I need you more than you can imagine. You are going to change everything and make this thing more real than just words on a page.'

The things Brian was saying were, understandably, disturbing Stephen. He decided he would interject to try and make the situation a little less frightening.

'Listen, Brian,' said Stephen trying to remain calm and bring Brian along with him, 'let's just both calm down. I am not saying that you can't choose to believe what you want to believe. But I just think that this might have all gone to your head. This is all being done to satisfy yourself.'

'No. I want to save those people.'

'Oh, don't talk bullshit, Brian. I thought that this was about money now, anyway.'

'That's just a happy bonus. The money is largely unimportant. It is the readership that I'm really interested in.'

'This is insane. You're insane!'

'Stephen! I am very seriously warning you!' and Stephen believed him. He had a vague inclination of where this was heading. He had one more thing to say to Brian.

'To fear truth is to be dead.' And, just as some more rain began filling up his mouth, he spluttered, 'We are nothing without choice.'

'I couldn't agree more, Stephen, because you have left me no choice,' said Brian. And it was at that moment that he pulled back one side of his long mac and revealed something glimmering very dimly in the latter stages of a lightning fork. It was the handle of a knife sticking out of his trousers.

'You might think this is a power-trip. But it's so much more than that. Because my real power lies here. I have to help those people. It is my duty. And you can share that, Stephen, because I am going to make you a martyr.'

Chapter 27

Stage Right

A lone man walks down a darkened, midnight street. The rain pounds, sending water droplets metres off the floor as it hits it. It falls as if it will never stop, hitting the man over and over so that it is all he can see or feel.

But then it does stop. The sky above now seems emptier as he looks up, that is, until the stars begin to glisten once more. He wipes the water droplets from his glasses, but he is only really able to smudge them into a watery mass. Inside his mac pocket a stained knife sits. He can feel it through the material, slowly rubbing against his leg with each step he takes.

He is thinking deeply as he is walking. Words are beginning to form in his head. Words he is slowly fostering so that he may release them on a page when he arrives home. The clearer sky is doing things to his mind.

He takes the opportunity to reach into his pocket to take a cigarette from a pack and he places the tip casually into his mouth. He drags a match across the rough surface of the match-box and lets it catch alight in his fingers. The flame causes a sudden brightness around the man's face as he raises it to the cigarette and breathes the hot air in.

The fire spreads with ease across to the cigarette paper and slowly works its way up towards his mouth as he takes his first full breath in through the tobacco. He grasps the cigarette between his index and middle finger and lowers it from his mouth as he blows the smoke into the night sky. It is then that he throws the match to the grass on his left.

It is the grass that lies in front of a desiccated old house that lies empty and broken. It is the same house that he had walked past several weeks ago around the same time of night. Actually, exactly the same time of night.

It was the same house that he had thrown his match in front of as he continued walking down the street smoking his cigarette. It was the same night that he had walked further down the street to see two boys in pyjamas sneaking out of a house with a small bag. The bag made a noise that resonated in the man's distant memories, the slow grinding sound of marbles rubbing together. The kind of sound that causes you to feel, in the way that smelling makes you taste. It is the kind of sound that interlinks your senses and brings your past back in a wave of memory. He had passed the boys just as they were settling on a spot on the pavement outside the house and he had disappeared around the curve of the street.

Behind him lay the beginnings of a small orange glow named Malcolm.

Epilogue

Of Endless Sorts

I t is the future. Not right now. Right now it is the present. Don't worry yourself, you didn't miss anything, it's still the present where you are. However, it is the future where I am. I can do that, by the way, I can be in the future. I'm not too much into the future. About two hundred years or so but the message of Mooranity has certainly grown.

Mooranity is a religion that is based around the story of a late and great man by the name of Stephen Moore. Even though I'm guiding you to the future, I don't want to reveal too much. I don't want to spoil everything because that would leave you with the benefit of hindsight well before you need it, and what kind of existence would that be?

The main reason I have been writing all of this was to stop myself from going mad, but it actually ended up making things worse. And, of course, it is also because this is all very important.

The story of Stephen Moore is one that centres on a bench. This may seem a little odd, that's because it is. Stephen Moore supposedly died fighting for the right to teach Mooranity in front of this bench. He was stabbed to death by an evil person of some kind. No one has ever been able to establish who it actually was but this unnamed person is certainly a villainous figure in the teachings of Mooranity.

The Bench is now sacred and lies in a holy temple. Only the Head Teacher of Mooranity is allowed to sit on it where, at times, Stephen can give him small portions of Truth to tell the world.

The story says that, when Stephen Moore died, he found his way up The Platinum Staircase and onto The Island. He is the only person that momentarily saw Absolute Truth and returned swiftly to the land of mortals to give us a small portion of it. This is the reason for his importance in these teachings. It is reported that his first word was 'Ouch!' and, so the story goes, he returned briefly to us and spoke his final words. These final words are sacred in the teachings of Mooranity and are often repeated at some of their grander ceremonies. They reveal as much truth as Stephen could manage in his final moments with the knife he had deep in his heart. It is the story of Love, Peace, Happiness and Goldfish:

Love, Peace, Happiness and Goldfish

Then everything was Golden.

*And Nature and I turned to one another and pointed
to the sky;
For oranges are not a paradox nor lemons.*

*But everyone moaned at the prospect and the prospect
felt offended and appalled and basket.
And they dipped their toe in the fountain of eternal youth
for fear of getting wet.*

*Is this a Bench I see before me?
A place which I once loved more than any other.*

*May it remain standing, proud through the trial of time.
And the sounds and the sights and the tastes and the smells
and the feelings made people say, 'five is too many,' and
the dogs said, 'woof'.*

*And a woman's voice sang through the wind from the
South.
'Don't talk to me that way, young man; use your mouth.'*

And he began to tell me a tale.
It was about him telling his tale.
It told of his life and his death yet to come and he truly
told it so well.
He told me of everything that had ever occurred and it
took him a lifetime to tell.

But everyone shuddered at the idea and the idea shuddered
back and everyone wondered why the world shook.
There is no sense in counting; counting is only for those
with something to fear or something to cook.

The water cascaded or, rather, it fell so a man said, 'I'll
call that a waterfall'.
Then a woman said, 'I thought of it first,' and she held
up her barrel to catch it all.
And they danced in the joy of the springtime and thought
of Love and Peace and Happiness and Goldfish and the
bottom of the ocean and corkscrews and waving and paper
and leaves and Autumn that follows Spring.

'Millions of what?' said a small child. 'You can be a
millionaire after a million breaths and a million steps
and a million handshakes.'
And he shook his hand in the air in disgust and anger
and chocolate.

A smile flew across the sky, a mile high smile, and it grinned at everyone and everyone grimaced and went inside but their insides were gone.

And so the quest had begun. They were to find the Staircase. Everyone packed their lives into a hanky on a stick and their insignificance revealed itself.
But one became an expert, an expert in expertise, which made him an expert expert. This made him jump, for he was an expert in jumping.

'No, no, no, no, no' muttered a small, old woman, 'this isn't how it was meant to be.'
And so she walked on her feet instead.

A man that could only count to five missed out four and went straight to six. He cheered but no one heard and he calculated to cut his losses with a knife.
But he changed his mind and he held on. If he let go then everything was lost: his rope, his shoes, his stick and his hanky.
The tree trunk creaked and creaked and snapped and creaked a little bit more and then he fell, screaming, towards inevitability.
'Only God can save me now,' he cried and he moaned and he screamed and he groaned and he would've whimpered but he didn't have time because he hit the ground.

And they all thought of Love and Peace and Happiness
and Goldfish.

A loud explosion made them run for their lives but their
lives had run too fast.
And most people ducked but some goosed and they all
wistfully looked into the future to see what it held in its
Platinum hands.

A young woman turned to the crowd that surrounded
To see her express what had made her dumbfounded
'Rhyme' rhymes with itself. Is that a coincidence?'
'Don't talk rubbish!' they screamed with insistence.

One man found a diamond and said, 'it's mine.' So he
opened a mine to find more and they glistened in the
moonlight as the rain dropped onto their pure surface.
But the mine collapsed.
The man is presumed dead, which is the 'Stage Right'
before definitely dead.

They fought for their rights and their wrongs and their
dignity and hypocrisy and the voice bellowed from behind
The mountains,
'You have no idea about the laws of the oceans or the
mighty hand that guides you there'.
They replied with something quite witty but it's hard to
remember exactly.
Nobody wanted to say what they all thought was true
and their false smiles wore thin in the sleet, 'my feet, they
are weary and my hands cannot hold. My teeth feel like
ice-cubes cracking my gums.'

But nothing could stop this incredible beast that tore
up what stood in its way until a small girl with eyes the
size of rubies shone them into its face. And his grinding
teeth stopped and he looked down in confused awe for,
he thought to himself, he had never seen eyes quite like
that before.

And the screams shattered glass on the sides of the streets
as the people all stared into space.
'From where do we come? And why are we here? And
what's this strange mark on my face?'
Their first two were answered with bellowing beauty but
the last one was too tricky to the taste.
And as everyone shouted in realisation, they thought of
their luck and their fortune and fate.

*And, after it all, a man sang from a rooftop and it was
all made clear.
'The reason we are here, is to find the reason we are here.
Our work here is done,' he said.*

*And, as the bearded man slid into his second death, he
glared with importance as he said,*

*'One must respect the Staircase and learn to wait,
For one could meet a most unhealthy fate.'*

*And their thoughts turned once again to Love, Peace,
Happiness and Goldfish.*

Then everything was silent.

For silence is golden.

*And all of the colours joined their fingerless hands to
create an
Enigma
Of endless sorts.*

Stephen Moore at The Bench

19th January 2009

(Definitely)

The story of The Platinum Staircase within the teachings of Mooranity says that anyone who tries to ascend the Staircase before their time in an attempt to find Absolute Truth will fall into an Eternal Sea where they will spend forever searching for The Island to no avail. Those that pass through correctly at the end of their mortal lives (after all of their funeral guests have confirmed they are no longer breathing, of course) will walk safely onto The Island and meet Stephen Moore and from him they will gain the full and unabridged version of Absolute Truth.

These teachings have found their way into the hearts and minds of many people, and have taught them the laws they choose to live by so that they may safely find their way to The Platinum Staircase and ascend it upon their death. Running, bounding, taking it three, four steps at a time, and answering every question they might ever have had by pushing open a single door.

It is said that one day someone will be chosen to do the unthinkable and ascend The Platinum Staircase, find The Island, and return back to the mortal land once more, bringing with them unabridged and Absolute Truth. This has yet to happen. But there are those that wait, and they are willing to wait forever, and they are filled with hope.

***

If you liked this book why not try...

The Naked Umbrella Thieves

Sergeant Cyrano O'Hara had lost the lost property cupboard. Its whereabouts were a mystery. In fact the entire police station had been behaving strangely of late. Corridors were there one day, gone the next. The downstairs hall sometimes ended in a motorway. The building had been rearranging itself ever since a conjuror had been locked up in one of the cells.

Sherlock Holmes never had to deal with this nonsense.

Times are tough for the men and women of Old Grethwick Police Force. As if one-legged murderers, ghoulish thespians, drug-dealing vicars and human-hating buildings aren't enough to deal with, someone has just made seventy-five politicians disappear. At least that last one has cheered everybody up a bit.

About the Author

Although Ian Wild is one of the world's leading authorities on naturist parasol kleptomaniacs, he would like to point out that he always showers fully clothed and does not have a criminal record. He has written comedy for Ireland's RTE Radio One and won awards for short stories – most recently the 2009 Fish International Short Story Prize, but only to take his mind off undressing Mary Poppins. He was not naked writing this book. He was wearing an umbrella which he found in the hand of someone who wouldn't let go until he bit their wrist.

Order from www.knightstone-publishing.co.uk